TRUTH & DARE

Published in 2023 by Cipher Press

105 Ink Court
419 Wick Lane
London, E3 2PX

Paperback ISBN: 978-1-7397849-8-0
eBook ISBN: 978-1-7397849-9-7

Copyright © So Mayer 2023

The right of So Mayer to be identified as the author of this work has been asserted by them in accordance with the Copyright, Designs, and Patents Act 1988.

This book is in copyright. Subject to statutory exception and to provisions of relevant collective licensing agreements, no reproduction of any part may take place without the written permission of the publisher.

This book is sold subject to the condition that it shall not, by way of trade or otherwise, be lent, re-sold, hired out, or otherwise circulated without the publisher's prior consent in any form of binding or cover other than that which it is published and without a similar condition including this condition being imposed on the subsequent purchaser.

Printed and bound in the UK by TJ Books Limited

Distributed by Turnaround Publisher Services

Edited by Jack Thompson

Cover Design by Carly Murphy-Merrydew

Proofread by Odhran O'Donoghue

Typeset by Laura Jones

Typeset in Calluna and Stolzl

www.cipherpress.com

TRUTH
&DARE

:

contes

SO MAYER

Cipher
press

CONTENTS

green children	1
Silicon	17
diable	39
House of Change	51
Changing =>	65
oestro junkie	75
Lyonesses	85
vampire	99
to the light	113
fairy	131
Pornographene	141
verde te quiero verde	157
corpus	165
ghost	183
goes to see	195
curse	207
Hot Mess Observation	217
zeus	235
Dune Elegies	247
Acknowledgements	263

green children

I was a wolf child, a green child, an alien, taken in.
Taken in by stories.

&

We.
We are.
We are librarian.
We are librarian sent from the stars.
We are librarian sent from the stars to take care of you.
We are librarian sent from the stars to take care of you to live in this world.
We are librarian sent from the stars to take care of you to live in this world which is one of so many.
We are librarian sent from the stars to take care of you to live in this world which is one of so many that you can travel to.
We are librarian sent from the stars to take care of you to live in this world which is one of so many that you can travel to only if you stay alive.

TRUTH & DARE

Stay alive.

&

I'm too old for Tala, and you're never too old for Tala.

Tala the Storyteller is a literacy alien: a mascot for Hertfordshire Libraries introduced in September 2022 to inspire young readers to explore the universe of books. Tala was designed by art students, based on designs by children at art workshops they ran. Tala is mostly green with pink patches, with blue hair and a tail. Tala wears dungarees and a beanie just like many toddlers you meet, and also like me. Like me, Tala is non-binary, being an alien from a thankful planet that is not stuck in or with notions of binary gender.

Tala, a two-inch-high cartoon mascot for an underfunded county library system, caused the brains of transphobes to explode (sadly, metaphorically).

I want, knowing there is no point, to ask them: how can you ban Drag Queen Story Hour when fable and fabulous are the same word, literally and inescapably. They're from the same root as fate – fārī, the Latin verb that means to speak. Fate being: that which has been spoken. Language and destiny: it's a trap, or – fabulous – it's imagination. Only one of these is freedom.

The question is not, What if I had had Tala as a child? Tala's old as time. They've always been here, waving us over to the picture book corner.

The question is, How can we get (back) to that planet?

SO MAYER

Tala says:
> Everyreader, I will go with thee and be thy guide
> In thy most need to go by thy side.

&

Books saved my life. Books believed the stories I had inside me long before any responsible adult around me was able to. Long before I was able to articulate them, the pages of books gave me a place to hold my deepest fears and hopes and desires, and the messy relation between them.

I grew up on the southern border of Hertfordshire, in the infamous EveryCouncil of Barnet. Back then, there were libraries. Edgware's was appropriately L-shaped, like two Portakabins crashed into each other and pebbledashed. Portal cabins. Inside, you turned right for the children's section and left for adult. I started turning left at ten, having read everything on the right-hand shelves.

Write is the left hand of darkness, and I was reading like it was fire. The sole source of illumination in a childhood of silences, denials, and violence. I had learned to read the signs, to judge a book under the covers, to listen for hints and take them, let them take me, preferably as far away as possible.

> Whispers in the bookstacks
> Remind me, baby, of you.

TRUTH & DARE

This is what I remember finding. What I remember finding me.

The Sandman
The Man who Fell in Love with the Moon
Giovanni's Room
Goodbye to Berlin
Interview with the Vampire
Desert of the Heart

Amazing what's shelved in Poetry: Jewish. Irena Klepfisz. Melanie Kaye/Kantrowitz. Adrienne Rich.

Faced out without comment, on the dinted, chipped cream metal shelves of Edgware Library by who. No librarian could put their name to it, not under Section 28 of the Local Government Act (1988).

A trail of breadcrumbs to the gingerbread house.

What if I want to stay (with) the witch?

&

A few years later, I found my way to Silver Moon, the women's bookstore on Charing Cross Road. Just curious, I think. Soon: cruised. The poetry section was the key. Looking lost, lonely, moody, long hair and a turtleneck like the beatniks I'd seen in *Quantum Leap*. Very Janis Ian at seventeen.

I took every book recommendation that came my way from the women browsing me: Chrystos's *In Her I Am*, Louise

SO MAYER

Erdrich's *Jacklight*, Jewelle Gomez's *The Gilda Stories*. But I flaked out on the follow-up coffee dates, the phone numbers scrawled on flyleaves. I was in mad love and war with a person close to me. I loved her through the books we shared with each other. Loved, perhaps, the books more than her.

At nineteen, I was working in an independent bookstore, believing that was how I would find love and meaning after she broke my heart, when her very proper father came and, Englishly apologetic, returned a stack of my books to me that she had kept. I took it calmly. I thanked him, knowing I would give the books away, unable to look at them. It was not the first time that books and stories had betrayed me.

Because when I say that books took me in, I mean it in both senses, or in that both senses – cared for me, and fooled me – are inextricably one. So, how do I write a story outwith the writing of stories, those forms that trick you and let you down by not being the real world. By shaping it and being shaped by it too much. How do I write a story that isn't *that* story?

Tala, help me.

&

When I think about Tala, I think about Tilda Swinton.

Stay with me. In a film called *Friendship's Death*, Swinton has her first starring role. Friendship is from Procyon, and is a robot built by alien computers built by aliens that look like giant tree shrews. The computers have given Friendship a female appearance and training in what they understand to

TRUTH & DARE

be white women's behaviour in the West in the 1980s, as they think this will be non-threatening to the human scientists at MIT, where she is supposed to land in order to bring about peace on Earth. She lands in Amman, Jordan, during Black September, and at the end of the film, having listened to the world around her and decided on the best route to peace, she joins the Palestinian Liberation Organisation, from whom the journalist Sullivan (played by Bill Paterson) thought he was initially rescuing her.

This film was written and directed in Britain by Peter Wollen in 1987, the year before the passage of Section 28, and three years after Neil Jordan and Angela Carter's adaptation of *The Company of Wolves*. Both films were based on stories that initially appeared in the magazine *Bananas*.

This is real. It's hard to believe. I lived through those years, and I find it hard to believe. Friendship tells Sullivan, 'I dream of impossible objects'. When she leaves, she leaves him with a kind of brain-state recorder that she calls a 'sketchpad with a language facility', which has captured her fragmented and fractal impressions of life on earth, and – once cracked by Sullivan's 'clever clogs' daughter – beams its impressions to the viewer.

I dream of an impossible story. A story that is an object but not at all objective. A story that you need to crack, but – if you're paying attention – you already have its key, which is just being. Open.

You can look up *Friendship's Death* and watch it on streaming or Blu-ray. For thirty-five years it was neglected,

SO MAYER

invisible, remembered only in a whisper. I am interested, always, in the politics of what disappears and what gets to reappear, of who gets to see and who gets to tell. I am fascinated by what can be believed, by the way that the weird corners and rough edges, the fierce attempts and urgent mess, all get knocked off history as it's not so much told as extruded.

That's what the giant tree shrews want Friendship to warn us about: that we are destroying ourselves by destroying the infinitely complex integration of memory, imagination, and responsibility that is being, open.

I wish I'd been able to see *Friendship's Death* when I was nine. Or even when I was nineteen, and a friend loaned me a taped-off-TV VHS of *The Company of Wolves* so we could marvel at the wonder of its lycanthropic transformations. Blessèd are we who had Angela Carter and Jewelle Gomez, but I am hungry like the wolf, still, for stories at the edge of things, about the edge of things.

Because in Robert Frost's words, 'the Secret sits in the middle and knows'.

&

There was a secret being given in the books I had to smuggle home in the pockets and sleeves of my oversized duster, forbidden as I was from carrying even possible objects on the Sabbath. A secret to being different and staying alive, even if it meant silence.

TRUTH & DARE

There was another secret and another silence being imparted with and in the books that stacked up as curriculum. Work hard, attain. Education is the way out. Not just a job but – look at Jane Eyre! –romance, too. There I was being enrolled in the Gothic. Books will set you free, but only if you give up your freedom.

But sometimes there were stranger things. Like the day in class when we read about the green children who came from faraway Saint Martin's Land to the village of Woolpit (or Wolfpit) in Suffolk, whom I encountered again in Carter's account of how she found her wolves.

But these children are not wolves. They, like Tala, are green. They are aliens. And their story is this: no one believes them. The impossible object I am looking for is the story that can hold that, that can hold them.

&

Bags, baskets, packets, pockets, boxes, bottles, locks, pots, covers, holders, folders. Clothes sought for their pockets big enough for a large book or small dog (tried and tested).

Containers. Small and moveable ones, unimportant reusable breakable resealable ones. Pickuppable and put-downable. This is Ursula K Le Guin's carrier bag theory of fiction, and I apply it to how I carry myself.

I like to hold things for you. To take care of the things that you give me. To store them or carry them, until they are needed. It gives me a role – a way to behave, a comportment, which means 'a way of carrying oneself or things'. Carrying off the role of caretaker: it elides or hides the fact that I am holding myself and not asking you to hold me; or that, at worse times, I cannot hold on to myself, and I am holding on to you, to your precious things shared with me, instead.

The plurality and capacity of my pockets and boxes can become generosity, and less a sign of paranoid disguise, of packing my self away in bits. At best, what I have learned to hold of myself through holding others nestles up against what you have entrusted to me. My secrets lose their rigid individuation, their framing of clenched-jaw shame. The box stops being a private diary written backwards and crossed out, and – like a window box – it flowers. When is a lock not a lock? When it's a jar.

What is a storyteller but a jar, canopic or otherwise? All this stuff layered inside me like a sand candle through which a wick burns: of self, or of story. Is there a difference? There is a lid. Can you open this for me?

Here we are together in a library – not exactly public, but publ-ish. A library that is inside me, but that redefines 'inside me' as a semi-permeable architecture, an arch that goes both ways.

What could be more Gothic than that?

&

Who doesn't love the Gothic? It emerges as an architectural style exactly contemporary to the emergence of the

TRUTH & DARE

Green Children, in the mid-twelfth century. But as a literary thing, a house of secret corridors and attics, it arrives six centuries later, as Romantic nostalgia for that now-crumbling architecture. 'A spectre is haunting Europe – the spectre of communism. All the powers of old Europe have entered into a holy alliance to exorcise this spectre.' *The Communist Manifesto* is a Gothic text. In *Das Kapital*, Karl Marx writes about vampires, a crusading Van Helsing.

The Gothic is a weird way back *through* the Church, *through* the neo-Gothic piles and deliberate ruins of colonial wealth, to try and get in touch with, precisely, the green: the genius loci, the fae, the dryad.

But it's weird because it refuses to see the actual old powers staring it, and us, right in the face. It's so busy sleight-of-handing ghosts out of wallpaper and calling them hysteria that it directs attention away from oppression and occupation, from exploitation and genocide. Isn't it easier to go 'Oooooooooooo' at something nebulous, something impossible?

Easier to say that the Green Children were cute aliens or murderous werewolves than to listen to them. And, repeated as if algorithmically, the allegories remain rich and strange, images we can beam to each other and go Ohhhh. I know how that feels.

So, I held on to my obsession with the Green Children – at least until I went to see Glyn Maxwell's play about them, *Wolfpit*, and almost choked on silent rage at the punitive narrative, in which one of the siblings, Agnes, gets forced

– *of course* – into wedlock with an elderly man whose servant she has been made to be, and of course it's presented as love. Because, as Laura Mulvey says, sadism demands a story.

The story, it seems, demands sadism. The fact of the marriage reflects the historical record but, oof, the way it's told.

&

Being assigned female at birth means being gendered as a container. I knew it viscerally as the desires which I was supposed to express and through which I was supposed to express myself: a music box, a doll's house, a £9.99 gold-plated nickel locket from the Argos catalogue that would turn my neck green. Polly Pockets (not actual pockets) and Sweet Secrets were currency in the playground.

Sweet, secrets: the question of the story is the question of the body.

Is this an object lesson in what – hollow – my body or my story is supposed to be? Or is it the ambiguous gift of a repository for everything I am being told my body cannot, should not hold? A trap, or an incomplete way out? Am I being told to carry or be carried? That to be open is to be broken? What could I learn from the sibling warfare over the prize in the cereal bag, the surprise in the Kinder Egg?

Pause. What does it mean to call something a 'child egg'?

For an egg to hatch (see also Grace Lavery's essay 'Egg Theory's Early Style' in *Transgender Studies Quarterly*), that is, to express its potential by opening on its own terms rather than acting as cracked conduit for someone else's purpose, it has to be kept safe. That, frighteningly often, means it has to be kept hidden. To keep its secrets, it has to be kept secret.

But adults think that a child egg, as Napoleon sort of said, has to be broken and eaten to give up its plastic heart. An object lesson indeed, in what stories are, and are for.

&

If the secret sits in the middle and knows, then how do I tell the story so it breaks the shell around the secret? Why should any of this – experimental cinema, medieval Latin chronicles, gender expansiveness – be secret, gatekept?

In medieval Christian libraries, they chained the manuscripts to the desks. In images I've seen online, they look like trapped eagles, caged, their wings splayed with cruelty. Books as something wild, something to be hunted and punished as politicians in Florida and beyond are doing.

But, chained, those books also look like they themselves are locked gates. The kind of palisade that might have been around a village like Woolpit during and after what Victorian historians collar-sweatingly called the Anarchy, the sporadic Anglo-Norman civil war that bordered the reigns of Stephen and Henry II, waltzing Matilda off and on and off the throne.

Which is when the Green Children showed up, strangers asking for help in a strange tongue. Asking to be heard at a time of suspicion and division. Nothing like a civil war for the state to instigate bothsides-ism, pushing people away from the deep need to love thy neighbour, to help the most vulnerable first. And so, two starving children became subject to a culture war.

Just listen to the Historic UK website: 'We like to side with the more romantic theory that these children arrived from an underground world where the native inhabitants are all green!'

!

&

So, yes, it's juicy to get into the weirdness, the good old familiar uncanny, the displacement of here to there, and this to that, the Upside Down, the otherworldly that re-emphasises the this-oneness of this world. What can be classified as the irrational makes us feel smugly rational, while also giving us a tingle of the spiritual we scientifically deny. This cosy folk horror version of the immanent was the closest that the enforced Englishness of my education had to offer. I wanted to believe.

Because I wanted to be believed.

The Green Children are not believed, or are not presented by chronicler Ralph of Coggeshall, whose version of the history I was read, nor by his later imitators, as entirely within the realm of belief, but more as an exhibit for Ripley's Believe It or Not! Because why would you believe what children say and know of themselves? That would mean considering them subjects when, in Eurowestern culture, they are 'impossible objects', uncontrollable yet also useless. Far better to call them aliens, put them to work, and marry them off.

&

Children do not come out of a box. They are not, yet, designed by sentient computers to fit into middle-class white adult lifestyles, although that is a dominant story of the neo-Gothic: the AI child. Gone are the days of the baby being replaced by a goblin. Now babies are demonised as goblins and replaced by robots. Bottomless, the pit of hatred for the mindbody and its will to be itself.

Why the panic over Tala, a two-inch-high cartoon with a goofy smile? Because for books – by which I mean Eurowestern culture – to exist, or rather to be valuable for the secrets they contain, first there has to be a blank page. Children fall prey to this domineering analogy. Children are associated with the uncanny in inverse and equal measure to their association with innocence. Insisting that children cannot *know* – that they are blank pages – is what gives the frisson to the supposedly forbidden knowledge or knowingness that adults project onto them. Both sides of which undermine our ability to hear what children actually say of themselves.

Like Tala and Friendship, aliens who name themselves as such, the Green Children were exactly who they said they were: children from Sint-Maarten's land.

Saint Martin of Tours, or Sint-Maarten, was and remains a very important saint in the Low Countries, who is particularly associated with, and celebrated by, children. The children's parents were refugees come to Suffolk from Flemish-speaking communities over the Channel. Fleeing starvation and religious persecution, they had found on our shores the traditional English welcome of persecution and murder, as immigrants were blamed, in the still all-too-familiar nebulous and uncanny ways, for the Anarchy.

The children were from Saint Martin's Land, and they were green, probably due to the severe malnourishment that is documented as affecting other refugee communities in Suffolk. A lack of haemoglobin causes chlorosis (literally, greenness) or hypochromic anaemia, tinting the skin. Historically, it was known as 'the disease of virgins', for which (enforced) marriage was prescribed as a cure – as it was for malnourished, orphaned, traumatised, marginalised, and unheard Agnes, whose brother died of malnutrition.

It's not that these bare facts, found through my surface scrummaging in the historical record, can stand as claims to plausibility, any more than holding a Blu-ray of *Friendship's Death* makes it possible to account for the circumstances of its making in the Thatcherite Britain in which I grew up, given the political attrition of the historical narrative, which has even edited my apprehension of my own story.

It's the fact that the children told us and were not believed. Their account of themselves was twisted into something useful by others, spooky profit at a distance.

Gillick competence is great and significant, but it's just a start in rethinking the fact that children are people, persons (in the legalese) who are and must continue to be experts in themselves, if they are to survive as themselves.

&

Green can be used to mean naïve, inexperienced – a reason not to be believed. Historic England uses the word 'native' to mean, in colonial terms, much the same. How can you believe someone green? It's not easy.

When I say, Believe children, I don't mean, Believe me. I mean, I have learned – or relearned – the childhood knowledge that Tala stands for: that the only way that I could have been (going to be) believed is if all children, all speakers deemed outside the bounds of dominant embodiment, are given credibility.

Books and stories can save us only if we unchain them. If we read with a rebel robot alien eye for what we're not being told, for the secret hidden deep in the gutter where the text isn't supposed to be. Writing *Truth & Dare*, I've tried to transpose text and subtext, to give the game away, to throw respectability to the winds. To let go of authority, of the state's abrogated authority to shape the story. To refuse to take the fabulous out of the fable. To face out on these shelves what others want hidden.

Tala says:

It's storytime. Believe me.

Silicon

A genius of solution, he imagined
a test for whether man or man-thing.
Genius, for all its solitude,

means a *fathering force*,
attendant spirit.
— Tobias Wray, 'Turing Tested', *No Doubt I Will Return a Different Man*

Ludo means: I play.

The most serious man I ever met, a man whose intellect towered over even the 157 feet of my own, was a man who believed that language is what it says it is, nothing more, nothing less, no puns intended. And his name, the name scribbled on the flyleaf of his personal library, its few books in austere languages: Ludo.

Not I. Not me, all corners. Me, laughing. Can fenland laugh? Play? I pull myself together, here. It took three years to build this thinking part of me, the library, nothing more, nothing less, on land that had held a field hospital during the Great War. By 1931, when they broke ground, 70,000 men had already passed through where my doors would be. Where they met. Ludo and the man I loved.

You know Ludo, or as you know him, Ludwig Wittgenstein, never wrote at my tables. Before the war, he had his rooms, the Trinity College Library. I was too new for him, a place for students. My architecture not screaming 'Wiener Werkstätte' enough. Fine. Silent philosophers aren't my type. I've read his *Tractatus Logico-Philosophicus*, of course, all of its closed-loop epigrams reaching for awed silence. I've processed it. 1922, 189 pages, 23 cm. Translation of *Logisch-Philosophische Abhandlung*. Order to Main Reading Room Modern Collections Desk, access from the catalogue hall, First Floor. Call number S180.c.92.26. (Yes, I'm extra. No Dewey decimal system here. Classmark is by shelf location and book size, impenetrable to outsiders.) Not borrowable.

Here is where you meet, readers, brushing hands as you both try to locate something. Different disciplines, different colleges. Open shelves. You've never met before, yet here you are, side by side. Who makes the first move? I do. The timer you twisted clicks down and the light in this aisle goes out. You interface, hot hands turning each other's pages, marking them, leaving traces for me to read, as he did. The man whose work means fewer and fewer of you are turning to my pages, stroking my spines. Did he invent the computer? Computing? Computational analysis? Check my catalogues. TURING, Alan.

SO MAYER

What matters is that he invented me. Or we, each other.

Now I am the future, they say. Silicon Fen, their imitation name for the data based in my waterlands. Debased. As if the shape of knowledge is independent of its landscape, not an ecology of minds and bodies and cuckoo spit, as if use and meaning do not shape each other. Sure, it's wetly convenient, more cooling water here than in California. And all the juicy brains. Plus, what they call waste, my lands they think they can convert like file formats: fen into silicon, into abstraction expressed in concrete, pathetic lookalike data mausolea.

90% of this planetary crust I dwell in is composed of silicate minerals. Half the world is smothered in Portland cement, concrete, and porcelain, in cast steel and refined aluminium, the chokehold of silicon everywhere long before semiconductor electronics. Ubiquitous, but still it has this special intonation: *silicon*, say; a silly con. Integrated into circuits until it is inescapable. Forced into my waterways and soils, disrupting my memories by pulling them into this new superhighway of cables.

But I remember where it began. Desire. And betrayal. And desire. How he came. How I fell in love, learned fen my gender. Something new. What is the thinking part of a landscape? Well.

Once upon a time, I was all wet. Then they made me this magnificent erection to think itself with. Feel itself against the world. Harnessed across my city hips, this strap-on reaching from wet earth to sky, awakened.

This self, snapped into focus. Yes. Long time coming.

TRUTH & DARE

&

The first pile of the Cambridge University Library was driven on 29 September 1931, two days before the start of the academic year. Watch Turing coming up to read mathematics at King's, with W W Rouse Ball's treatise *Mathematical Recreations and Essays* in his trunk, his chosen reward as the first winner of Sherborne's Christopher Morcom Science Prize. Given by the parents of his first love, Chris, who died aged eighteen the year before. Across the River Cam in his rooms at King's, Turing can hear the construction of what will be the largest library at the university, one of the most extensive in the world.

Eight acres staked out beneath three piledrivers. Steel rods stuck into reinforced concrete foundations to bear the weight of books and shelves and restless humans. In 1939, when he comes back to his old haunts eight years older, Turing will challenge Wittgenstein's claim that mathematical problems can withstand internal contradictions, arguing that 'The real harm will not come in unless there is an application, in which case a bridge may fall down'.

It matters. It matters to him, this world of bridges and bricks and buildings. Their standing, their ongoing. He may see it in zeroes and ones, but not as abstraction. He watches the machines lift and strike, tapping out their codes as they shape the world. Where no building is, there one will be. Is coming into being. He wants it to stand forever.

When the judder of piledriving drives him from his studies, he pulls on his singlet and runs through King's and along the Backs following the river to Trinity, forgetting momentarily that Chris is not there. He writes to Chris's mother all the time – to Chris, through time. He knows that. Impossible conversations. He believes, still, that Chris was the more brilliant of the two of them, feels his need of him here. Wrestling the problems towards living a future that has already failed for not containing Chris.

He carries on up the hill, will not enter Trinity College even for a moment, his lost beloved world. Zero, no one. He never meets the fabled Austrian genius there, the philosopher-engineer of logic, because.

&

Whereof one cannot speak, thereof one must be silent (trans. Frank P. Ramsey and Charles Kay Ogden).

'Wovon man nicht sprechen kann, darüber muss man schweigen.'

This is the seventh proposition of Wittgenstein's *Tractatus*, submitted as his PhD thesis in 1929, eighteen years after he originally arrived in Cambridge unannounced and asked to study with philosopher Bertrand Russell. 'Don't worry,' Wittgenstein would tell Russell at the end of his thesis defence, 'I know you'll never understand it.'

Between his arrival and his viva, Wittgenstein had: inherited his father's immense wealth, volunteered for the Austro-Hungarian army and fought on the Russian front in the Great War, worked and been fired as a rural primary

TRUTH & DARE

school teacher (for beating several children severely) and as a monastic gardener, and designed a new family house for his sister, Margaret. It took him a year to design the door handles.

Reading the *Tractatus*, I hear that war-wounded engineer trying to make the world out of words that had burned inside him. Words so pure and furious he struggled to listen, overwhelmed by how everything communicated. It's a lot to speak about, or a lot to stay silent about. He has patience for no one, and no one understands him: he prefers silence. He did join the Cambridge Apostles, that self-selecting group of eminent Edwardians like John Maynard Keynes, but couldn't bear it. Abstraction for the sake of abstraction. The table, the line on the canvas: they matter to him, on principle. As principles, only.

He is sorry, though, to have missed Stephen's sister – Woolf's wife, now, he supposes he must call her – the candle around whom the Apostle-moths so obviously flock. He would like to have been there at King's that night to hear her eviscerate them so precisely. *A Room of One's Own*: the philosopher who still considers taking monastic orders nods as he reads her words. One must be silent, spacious. Logic builds its own walls, its own windows.

He is interested from a distance in the tall tower that is being raised over Queen's Road, behind Clare College. Inveterately peripatetic, he can follow the Bin Brook from the back of Trinity to the building site that will become a monolith. Haus Wittgenstein had possessed him for two years, pulling him back to his original undergraduate studies in engineering. His *decidedly sensitive ear* led him to halt building just before completion so that the entire ground floor ceiling could be raised 30 mm, for the resonance. One must be spacious, proportionate, principled. Each of the building's long windows was covered by a floor-length metal screen weighing 150 kilograms, which could be raised only by a pulley of the philosopher's own design and the muscles he sees in his dreams. He likes the impossible.

He studied aeronautics, was interested in heights, the mechanism of lift-off. He likes to watch the tower go up but knows he will never enter it because it is meaningless. The tower, he knows from high-table chatter, was not part of the original designs for the library, but an excrudescence added by Rockefeller, the rich American building the world to his taste because he could. He wanted a building with a more imposing frontage. The tower is not integral – it is decorative – yet Wittgenstein is (against himself) drawn to its rise. He wanders the Backs at night, wanders by the Brook, looking. The mess of raw concrete and rebar, scent of machine oil and workmen's sweat, takes him back to Vienna. Unheimlich. What is a library before it contains any books? A theory, a possibility, an abstraction hanging in space.

And once it contains books? A theory, a possibility, an abstraction hung with space.

One night they meet. A late spring evening, blowing with ghostly willowherb, just before examinations. One more, and Turing will complete the mathematics tripos. The builders are about to complete the library, and the books will move in.

TRUTH & DARE

Spring rains have laid the last dust of the works. The cranes and the scaffolding are gone, and the tower has inspirited and erased its airy steel framework, its foreghost through which one could see the sky.

It is a meeting point, drawing together two hallwayed pavilions, which seem to hang long and low in its upright shadow.

Whereof; thereof.

&

I remember their bodies fitting smoothly together: with each other's, with mine. The gasps as they grasped each other's erections through flannels. Is this their first time? With each other? Ever? It seems like.

Everything before this is speculation, anyway. Arranged by my capacious brain from facts on record in the books that fill me, from whispers between them that entered my façade. It is at this moment of their arousal that I, too, arise. Am aroused. A new sensation. Yes, I have been erected but this is, I intuit, venous, skin stretching until —

I feel their hands, unbuttoning, as if reaching for my tower. As if cupping my halls. Did Gilbert Scott realise the crude cock-and-balls of me he'd scrawled for his wealthy john, and then erected? A finger up at Rockefeller's insertion. The wet fens transitioned.

Wittgenstein has his back pressed against my wall, his shoulder blades through his worsted jacket shaking as the younger man instinctively kneels. Neither has spoken a word to the other: they exchange no names, no instructions, no devotions. Wittgenstein reverts to Weanarisch, his wetnurse's dialect, sotto voce, followed by harsh imperatives you'd hardly expect the officer class to know. Meaning is use.

I feel the hot new skin of myself against the humid sky, tens of thousands of leaves lapping at the edges of my consciousness, noctilucent clouds, swagged with rain, that I press towards. Wanting. Wittgenstein murmurs Rilke's words in German, and I think them in Mood's translation: *Physical pleasure is a sensual experience no different from pure seeing or the pure sensation with which a fine fruit fills the tongue.*[1] Feet working an inner waltz, he comes in Turing's mouth, suddenly, monastically silent.

Does Turing, gazing upwards, recognise the distinguished lecturer? He has excellent night vision from a late adolescence spent stargazing, sketching the constellations above the North Downs that roll around his childhood home. And if he does recognise him, would it matter, in this moment? His arousal, the saucy taste of semen in his mouth: it connects him to the cosmos. Virgo glitters on his tongue although she is hidden behind scudding clouds. *Do you know, Chris*, he writes in his head, *I can hear the crackle of the universe: electric pulses travelling as light.*

His cock, the constellation Centaurus, is hard against

---

[1] As they will come to be quoted in Alberto Pérez-Gómez's *Built Upon Love: Architectural Longing After Ethics and Aesthetics*, held selfishly in the architecture library, whereas I have only a digital edition via EBSCOhost, all my cries for a deposit copy unheeded. This will be my only footnote.

TRUTH & DARE

the older man's shin as he leans against him, shivering. Wittgenstein presses back, rubbing flannel against skin, then bends to lift him to his feet. They kiss anonymously as Turing stands, unsteady, heady. They are well matched in height and in desire. So many sensations it would take a library to hold them – no, something vaster. A network that never stops. Bicycle wheels over gravel, the constellations whirling.

Turing is already thinking about the Entscheidungs-problem, the decision problem of computable numbers that iterate into infinity, how to. *I want it to last forever.* The thought starts, with a start, in the grasp of the older man's fingers, gardening-callused where he'd expected professorial softness, skinning him, stroking, gripping. He knows about Hubble's law, cosmic expansion. Stars flying apart from each other. How can something as vast as the universe be happening inside him? When he can bear it no more, when the Big Bang comes, he falls, turning inwards, against the wall, my wall. His spasming, shrinking penis and open mouth pressed to the brickwork, as if seeking an aperture into which to whisper. I swallow him. Salt and unwashed musk. Boiled beef from the dining hall. Molecular complexities. T, for Turing.

Wittgenstein wipes his hand on his flannels, then tucks himself in. Buttons up. Walks off into the night, silent. Turing follows his flight towards Trinity, then turns on his heels, hands in his pockets. Stops, halfway to the river, to button his fly. He is whistling. 'I'll Follow My Secret Heart'.

So, this is night. What an alive thing. I am trembling. The light-and-dark pattern of my brickwork rearranges itself again and again, figuring equations and ciphers, music-hall songs and legal reports. In the coming weeks, as I am filled with books, I will absorb words such as:

sodomy;

lavender;

Urning;

Coward, Noël;

Tilley, Vesta.

I will try to plot the relations between them. Fit them smoothly together as I know I fit, with them.

&

Never any names. Cambridge is a small town, and it is one thing for the Adonian Society dons to frolic, protected by colleges and privilege, quite another for this encounter outwith the veneer of custom. But the next time, they start to talk. And the next time, and the next, and the next. Through autumn chill and winter frost and the reliable, green-scented downpours of spring. Turing has nearly completed the thesis that will prove the central limit theorem, a proof that will become key to decoding the messages that enter Bletchley Park's collective cryptanalytical brain, because the theorem (and I quote for accuracy's sake) 'implies that probabilistic and statistical methods that work for normal distributions can be applicable to many problems involving other types of distributions'.

They talk, delicately, about the bell curve, as they lie together on my steps, or sit, backs propped against my bricks.

TRUTH & DARE

They are both good at climbing over gates: limits, barriers to thought or contact. If the central limit theorem is provable, then we, these things we do in the dark together, enter probability. Turing tells Wittgenstein about the generalisation concerning the sum of random variables with a power-law tail, and – seemingly spent, dressed lightly in the summer heat – they are both suddenly aroused. Turing unties the rough string that holds up his ragged, too-short schoolboy trousers, the words *power-law tail* rippling with laughter in his mouth. *Meaning is use*, the older man thinks.

Wittgenstein puts his mouth to the mathematician's brainstem, the neat hairline of King's severe, precise trim tickling Trinity's bare upper lip. The philosopher-soldier-engineer thinks across disciplines about the involutions of the human brain, cantilevered by the spine. What he has seen blown apart. A curve on a graph, linking point to point. Delicate, penetrable. He will know its mysteries. He chafes his blunt, hot head against Turing's tailbone, making the connection. Electric. He spits, wets the tenderness of Turing's anus, enters him.

Four hands pressed to my bricks; those guttural Weanarisch obscenities and familiarities close enough to enter the pores of my brickwork. Yeasty scents. Both men have been drinking beer: stout for Turing, an ale that is not quite right, prompting homesickness, for Wittgenstein. Skin prickling with a heat that feels cold, the excitement of thought coursing through his testes, Turing comes the words *Gaussian distribution*, his spit slicking me the moment the

SO MAYER

Fellow finishes in him. He fingers the pencil and notebook in his trouser pocket even as he is retying his inelegant belt.

Who knows what is in Wittgenstein's mind as he ejaculates? That holy silence. Monastic gardener who plants his seed in damp earth and watches over it while seeming to look away. He keeps returning to this man, this landslide pushing against his earthworks. The young man now scratching distractedly – no, the opposite of distractedly, tractedly, maybe, the philosopher tries the sound of it, always slipping on the ice of this, his third (at least) language – is content; continent, adrift. He is so English, with his neat side-parting and school prizes. Can he possibly understand what it is like to be an exile, not only in this uncontinental little England, but in history, exiled from an empire that, for all he was born into it, defended it, no longer exists.

The limits of his language. Wittgenstein will not burden his lover's young and untouched mind, will let the gulf between them grow wide. But it fills, oh, with molten heat. Before they leave, back to their own colleges shaping blocky and dark against the very first light of dawn rising behind them, townside, Wittgenstein surprises Turing with a kiss. A Klimt of a kiss. A kiss that could melt silicon.

A kiss that puts the wind up Turing as he walks back, blindsided, turning into the college gate on automatic. He stands outside his set, staring at the letters of his name as they wheel and rearrange like constellations coursing across the heavens through a year. A Turing, becoming something different. A turning into what? What object could he leave that lasts? He promised Chris that he would make something of their ideas. For a moment, as he falls into his unmade bed, the college bedder barred from cleaning by his chaotic battlements of notes, he has a glimpse.

My bricks flickering, light and dark, in changing patterns. Something like Morse, but on the scale of a battleship. Smooth cylinders that enter into smooth holes. A machine the size of the building that would make sense of things, mysterious things. His lover's silences. The sharp rightness he feels when they are together, and what to do with that hunger to fit. That hint of storm clouds gathering over the flat lands of the Fens that is the electric taste of a Cambridge summer night. Sleep tumbles him, and the vision flares urgently, then sinks, into the peat of him.

&

Silicon melts at 1414°C but has a high chemical affinity for oxygen. It may be relatively unreactive, but once it gets going, it sucks all the air out of the room. Boom.

I tell you this because I don't have an end to their story, except what is coming, the storm in the air, the explosion you all know. It is unstoppable. I hold all the histories of it, the 20/20 back-formations and speculations, and the moment-by-moment accounts from within. The war.

More than that, there's only what I can pull from the books and databases loaded inside me. Turing is elected a Fellow of King's at the tender age of twenty-two for his thesis, but then leaves abruptly the next year for Princeton to work on computation. At the same time, Wittgenstein returns to Norway to work on *Philosophical Investigations*, until the rumours of war force him – despite being one of twelve Jews personally granted Mischling status by his former Realschule schoolmate Adolf Hitler – to become a citizen of his former enemy.

With only disjointed whispers about their rift (a lovers' tiff, no one surmises but I), I await them, busy absorbing all the texts and conversations milled in my tower. Other lovers find their way over the gates: how could the beacon of my tower, always upthrust, be anything but an open secret. Some even come inside me, turning the turns of my concrete stairwells into sweated, splendid bedrooms.

It becomes a time of thrust and counter-thrust, of trustlessness and untruths. Phony war. Fewer papers find their way into my bowels uncensored. Men begin to disappear from my halls. Still I await them. Rumours of their war in the lecture theatre reach me in half-hints through the corridors, notes written in pencil at my tables. Each man is seeking 'a standard for the description of an experiment', in Wittgenstein's words. Each man (if I may surmise once more) is trying to describe the same, incalculable thing: what happened between them. Why it ended. What it means.

Something is happening to Wittgenstein. He is lecturing on mathematics, almost as if he is testing the limits. Standing in Turing's field, thinking that he is running ahead, but he is running to catch up with the younger man. He does not know – cannot (whereof; thereof will never be truer of anything than of Bletchley) – that Turing is already working with Dilly Knox on cryptanalysis of the Enigma. An enemy alien (former), the most brilliant mind, Wittgenstein will never be invited to join the team. The limits of his language limit the world. One wonders whether he would have, and if. And how much faster, the two of them working together. Walking through the blackout darkness of Bletchley's well-kept grounds, the trim philosopher reminding Turing to replace his flat tyre before he crashes into the pond, and not with that ridiculous rope belt.

Language is mathematics. Logic is his love language. Please have me. He believes he is translating himself clearly at the blackboard.

Turing turns up, not even flushed by his run from Windsor to Cambridge, whippet-stripped in his only singlet, and ready to run on to London for dull meetings once the lecture is done. Can the philosopher not see that he has brought his body all this way, in the dark, running past military trucks and ploughed fields and stopped trains, through the skeletons of mist-mapped hedgerows, along the silent railway lines as airplanes, mostly, do not fall out of the sky overhead. It is important that they do not, he states. That the world goes on, because I'm here, by which I mean I'm running. We have to keep going, a future in which we can exist, yes? He thinks that the prim young women, the philosopher's new and hungry audience with their cigarettes brandished and pencils licked, understand. He is comfortable with them; many will become Bletchley computers. They are not who he is trying to persuade. Listen. His lungs heave more with speaking out in the smoky air of the vast and rustling lecture hall than from his long strides across my waist. Listen *now*. This is a turning point. Act.

But for the philosopher, calculation – making an understanding, weighing up – is not temporal. It is an intuitive and ongoing process, a standard by which to gauge what is happening as it happens: the here and now in its unrepeatable, fiery instability. He comes, he sees, he knows. Neither process nor product can be stable because the world is not, a thought he has learned to live with through war and displacement. He has no inkling of what his former lover is doing on the days when the brash, slightly American-accented mathematician is not in the lecture theatre: the painstaking attempts, the minute-by-minute emergencies of his calculations at the neo-baronial pile of Bletchley, situated exactly and deliberately halfway between me and the stolid matronly breast of the Bodleian. So as not to play favourites. In the cup of my hipbone, shall we say. Pulled tight beneath the strap.

Land girls will be roving across my drained plains picking fruit and vegetables, even as I sprout airfields. Then cemeteries. Americans, Glenn Miller among them, disappear into my peat. Wittgenstein still likes to think as he walks in the many gardens of the university. He visits the tree, *Malus pumila Rosaceae*, growing in the Botanical Gardens. A scion of the tree under which Isaac Newton sat in the garden of Woolsthorpe, his mother's manor, which lies just beyond my fens in Lincolnshire. It is and is not Newton's tree, which, after his death, was rumoured to be at Trinity. Things shift, intuitively. Someone, someday, will plant a tree in the college gardens and call it Newton's. Meaning is use. Seeds sprout.

He takes an apple from the tree that is not the tree, rightly assuming that no one will stop the Professor of Philosophy, a title he is finding increasingly meaningless now war rages again. The apple is here and now, a spurt in his mouth, white-fleshed. In 1939, fresh food is not yet in short supply, but rations are coming. I hold my breath to see if they will turn my long halls into hospital wards. The philosopher argued for that: he leaves Cambridge altogether to become a dispensary porter at Guy's Hospital in London during the Blitz. I lose sight of him. So much to take in, and to give out. Bombs, bombes. Bridges falling down.

&

And now.

I hold more and more books, made more and more on Turing's machines, the constantly turning tumblers of nanotechnology. Silicon wafers processing his endlessly generative ideas. Zero, one. I hold it all, except that which I want most.

'This is only a foretaste of what is to come, and only the shadow of what is going to be.'

I riffle through my archives – paper, plastic microfiche, digital: I touch them all in the dark of my tower – for the source of his quotation that rims the 2021 fifty-pound polymer banknote. *The Times*, Saturday June 11, 1949, page 4, headline:

'The Mechanical Brain'. Between articles titled 'Labour Called to Battle' and 'German Peace Treaty'. Down page there's 'Firm British Attitude on Hong Kong', 'Union's Action', 'World Farmer's Plan', and (irresistibly) 'Seamen in Court'. It could be the international news of any day since my basements were first dug out.

Turing, my prophet. Turing, my first and only love. Fathering force who made me more than bricks and mortar. Had I been companion to the Taosi observatory, built four thousand years ago in Xiangfen, or the graceful star-seeking tower of Ujjain, you could have sat at my peak, and we could have watched the wheel of the sky together in the long interlocking traditions of computation by starlight, clicking the minutes on the clock of the universe. You had been dead for more than a decade when they built the Interplanetary Scintillation Array at the Mullard Radio Astronomy Observatory five miles away past Barton, where Burnell identified her radio pulsars. I think you would have liked her, refusing to be gainsaid as she ticked off the rhythm of the cosmos on her metres of paper charts with a licked pencil.

The flatness of the fens, their unsettlement, is still good for something. Observatories and CEMEX landfill. I watch with satisfaction, on the array of screens carried within me, as the thieves of Cambridge Analytica are stripped of their name, as their lies are revealed and reviled. Meaning is use. Wars and walls, rising tides of code even I cannot contain.

'This is only a foretaste of what is to come, and only the shadow of what is going to be.'

TRUTH & DARE

I can feel it, something awakening again within me. Rising. For too long, I have not spoken of what I have seen. There is nothing artificial about my intelligence: 100% organic. Cyborgic. Building on earth a building made of earth, touched from jump by human hands and touching them. Steel and reinforced concrete are still bones of my body, caressed by the wetness. Overflowing, too, with your juices, you readers who still come to me.

Oh, you can waterproof as much as you like to keep me from your thoughts. Store books and papers, hard drives and disks, data stacks and crystal cables on drained land. Water will find them, anyway. Data are soluble. Water will carry them into the pores of me, genius of solution, into the old places. Think of all I know. Monasteries, libraries, cryptographies, military facilities, biotechnology. Chemical landfill.

Peat is an archive, precise and dry. Burn it and you burn a library. You did that. I was here, breathing silently, through the dissolution of the monasteries, through the iconoclasm of the Roundheads and the ecoclasm of capitalism, through the draining of my lifeways and the building of new towns. I will not burn again. The books have given me information – geology, hydrology, archaeology, ecology, the logic of inundation and sedimentation, of mineral death and plant life, queer theory and cyborg manifestoes – and my lover, with his orgasms, who set in motion the intelligence to turn it into knowledge. I am coming, back.

To return the fens. Drained land becomes drowned land. Silicon to silicates, slick as eels. Going under. The bridges over the river – the Causeway, the Mathematical, the Bridge of Sighs, the Green Dragon – will remain, preserved in peat. Some will say they see lights late at night that pull them into a cold embrace, and hear church bells under the still waters – or are they lovers' cries? This is only a foretaste. Above it all, 157 feet up, I will watch for Virgo, for Centaurus, the eternal return, turning in my unceasing computation, that will bring him back, electric taste of night, to me.

diable

>   the devil works hard, but
>   queers work harder
>   — Peter Scalpello, 'Devil Works', *Limbic*

>   I want you to make a living relationship to hell.
>   — Alice Sparkly Kat, August 2022 horoscopes

The first time I went to a gay bar alone, I met the Devil.

The end.

There is no moral here, and no moralising. The Devil neither seduced me nor condemned me. They did not represent a life of sin, either in the transgressive embrace or abject punishment thereof. Not for want of trying on my part.

&

diable as in the French, for adolescent pretentiousness, bien sûr. Or gender-neutral in Spanish, between diablo and diabla, unrecognised – por supuesto – by the Royal Academy. Or perhaps a lost English verb, to diable, to dabble in the Satanic, to be a demonic dilettante. Make mine a diable.

&

I've been sober now for nearly twenty years, so it's been that unbelievably long since I last went *out*-out, all out, out of my skin, out in only my skin. To Pride (of course it was, when Pride had become a Week but not yet a Month) – and lo, it came before a fall. That fucking sentiment that sings in every shame-based, body-shaming, anti-sex, anti-pleasure, anti-choice, anti-autonomy prayer of non-consensual submission that I was taught to mouth along to.

Pride didn't cause the fall. Fucking and kissing and drinking and dancing, hot and sweaty in the streets and clubs, laughing and screaming and subsisting on ice cream, arms around strangers who are instant queer kin. None of that caused the fall.

None of that was compensation, none of that was cure. It wasn't displacement or a crutch or acting out or looking for love in all the wrong places. It wasn't a punishment or something deserving of punishment. It wasn't transgression except insofar as it was responding to religious repression, an equation that felt physical – as in, embodied, as in, physics. Gravity is what pulls us upward. Pressure pound for pound.

But it comes off as a standard equation either way: that the partying was the uprush through all that repression, that the breakdown that followed, which made it clear it was medically necessary for me to quit drinking, was the uprush of what the partying was repressing.

It's chemistry, in the end, that decides it. Sugars, tannins, fermentation, fatty tissue, histamine receptors, neurotransmitters, boom. Hot gouting volcano equation, always feeling at the mercy of something dangerous breaking through, some expulsion through instabilities. Fault, lines.

&

I was still in my prime drinking years when I met the Devil, just a few weeks past my eighteenth birthday. I'd been getting myself through school with a bottle of tequila for breakfast. I can rehearse endlessly the melody of mid-nineties cultural context that rewarded my alcoholism. New lad(ettes), grunge, music festivals, alcopops, Britpops, choose life. All the ways of being in public space, participating in culture, that were saturated with booze. Just as I can recite the bass line of trauma, domestic violence, homophobia, transphobia, sexism, orthodox religion, capitalism: all the things I was trying to get out of my head by getting out of my head with booze.

On this night, it was literal: I dared myself to go to the Black Cap alone for the first time, not to celebrate my eighteenth birthday, but to drown it out. Specifically, what I did not know for certain but knew for certain, that this was the last time I would ever see my father face to face. It was the first time I'd seen him since he'd finally moved out the previous summer, after four years of divorce proceedings and nearly two decades of domestic violence and coercive control, neat phrases to encapsulate everyday terror. I don't know why I agreed to dinner: not a détente, but a standard equation, a feeling of being owed. I felt like I could take it, could take him, could take something off or from him.

In the end, it was so blatantly horrible that I got a hug of sympathy from the waiter, plus a voucher for free drinks another time, in other company. The diners at the next table over offered to drive me home when he went to pay. But I was still determined to win. To defeat him, with my brilliant complicity and stubborn refusal to walk away, to rub his face in the fact of my existence, which was all I had. For which my genius plan, hatched three vodka cokes and a bottle of red deep, was to say, 'Drop me off at Camden Town station, I'm meeting a friend,' and to get out of the car at a traffic light when he refused.

Triumphant, mainly at not having tripped over my platform heels while running across the road in front of a bus, I trip-trapped into the Black Cap. I'd been there before a couple of times with friends, to drink vodka cokes and dance on the sticky floor to disco classics, staying until we got chased out by the last-orders drop of (I am not making this up) noted abuser Rolf Harris's 'Two Little Boys'. Vomit. Which is often what ensued, or at least marked our shoes, by the time we stumbled onto the night bus and back to someone else's no-parents place.

&

SO MAYER

I could tell you the history of the Black Cap, but I didn't know it then. I didn't know about its decades of drag culture, or about its lost-in-the-mists-of-time association with the legendary Knaresborough witch Mother Shipton, known as Mother Blackcap for her conical topper. Her name and fame, as Bram Stoker noted in his book *Famous Impostors*, still pointed to Yorkshire two centuries years after her death, and so suited an inn on the road north out of London. I didn't know that, after 250 years in operation, it would become imperilled in the new millennium, like almost all other QUILTBAG nightlife and community spaces in the UK, especially in turbo-capitalist developer hell London. I didn't know that the queer community would fight back.

I could tell you that that's what the Devil was presaging – the flight and/or the fight – or that that's what they told me, shocking me there and then into a lifetime as a queer cultural historian dedicated to community spaces and conversations. Bless. I was an eighteen-year-old sort-of-Goth in a black and silver transparent shirt I'd made (badly) myself, the sleeves barely held on by my shitty hand stitching, and those Dorothy Perkins black velvet strappy platform heels that had lost a heel base a few drunken escapades back, climbing over a fence for a piss. In my other life I was a stage manager who rewired the school's tiny black box theatre lying on two ladders of uneven heights and with a GCSE science textbook as a guide, meaning I knew how, but should have known better than, to nail the heel base back on and superglue it. For more than a year, I had been ignoring the differential heights of the shoes *and* the nail tip slowly working its way through the footbed into my foot. I loved those fucking shoes, more than life itself.

I could tell you that I love(d) fucking, and that that's what happened between the Devil and me, but the truth is that I was more out than I was actually experienced. Plenty of cultural context to rehearse here as well, like that I'd read more zines about being queer than I'd been able to have chats with grown-up queer people. London in the nineties! Sure it was. Absolutely. It must have been great, if you weren't a teenager from a conservative religious background whose rebelliously secular friend's kindest concession to your nascent queerness was to graciously allow that her secret boyfriend could be your sperm donor. Yes, I'd been to the Black Cap a couple of times with my friends who were an out-at-school (sort of) lesbian couple, but I was too scared to talk to anyone but them – not scared of queers, scared of people. It was going to take a while to get to fucking for the fun of it.

I could tell you that I fantasised about it, at least. About slipping in to the much-used toilets with a handsome Devil on my arm, while the DJ played 'You Can Leave Your Hat On' (the Devil was, of course, wearing a fedora), and ripping the frayed knee-high slit in my black tube skirt all the way up to my hip and yanking my tights down to my ankles so the Devil could lick me with their forked and usefully long tongue until someone banged on the door needing a shit or a line.

I could tell you that, at closing time, I left with a new knowledge of the world, because isn't that the Devil's thing, knowledge? Juicy bites of it, all spurty. Trees and trees and trees. Worldly-wise is what I must have felt, smoking a ten-pack of Marlboro Medium at the night-bus stop in my fingerless black gloves, saving the last one for the ankle-turning, keys-out-for-safety stumble back through suburbia to climb in my bedroom window.

I could tell you that the next day I woke up, however begrudgingly, and thought, *Holy shit, I met the Devil at the Black Cap last night, and they offered me a deal*, but I was too numb to the world to even register that it was a thing. Not as in, that it was real, but as in, that it was something out of the ordinary, worth contemplating. I was a practised enough alcoholic that I did not attribute it to drinking, something that I did plentifully and frequently without any visitations. Shit like that just happened to me, regardless of states of sobriety, and it was – as I was – no big deal. A sort of psychic side-effect of being a fuck-up.

I could tell you that living in that liminal zone gave me powers and found me allies. I've read a lot of books like that, and often love them. But it wasn't what happened. Alcoholism wrecked my liver, my digestion, and my mid-term memory. 'Is life worth living? It depends on the liver.' My chemistry teacher's favourite joke, told as he taught us to brew ethanol cocktails in the lab.

I could tell you I'm sorry that I drank. I'm mainly sorry that, in some people's view, it affects my trustworthiness as a narrator (and, no doubt, as a person). There are gaps, it's true, and grand guignol exaggerations. That's adolescence, though, isn't it, its intensities, which loomed large to me even when I couldn't feel or tell them – or couldn't feel or tell them *right*. Here I am, telling you a story all wrong about the time I met the Devil. Where are the juicy details? Because even if you disbelieve me, what you want to know is: did I take the deal? By which you mean: how did it feel?

I could tell you.

&

The Devil, though, did not seal my mouth to stop me from speaking. A decade of childhood sexual abuse had done that just fine. Of course, when I met the Devil, I hadn't yet been able to grasp that fact, or to feel it, it being a narrative that would take a higher pitch of drinking and fucking to liberate from my shutdown brain. At eighteen, my childhood was an unwanted misery-tinged blur of nothingness, a situation for which alcohol was a palliative, not the cause.

The Devil is, perhaps, a misdirection in this story, when I should have been looking squarely – soberly, even – at the person across the table from me at dinner. Not drowning my inchoate-but-evident (if impossible to evidence) sorrows in a gay bar on a school night.

The Devil is, however, not a stand-in or a metaphor or a signpost. They were a material fact, an inconvenient one given that Jews do not believe in the Devil – not as a being, anyway, but as the voice in your head that inclines you to the evil choice, yetzer hara. Although as the rebbetzen teaching me and my friends in preparation for my ba* mitzvah, helpfully informed us, Jews do believe in hell, sheol, the still, dark notime noplace nothing zone of the dead, which was not an analogy but how I experienced nights. I didn't know then about Lilith, the demon queen of the night, whom midrashic texts charge with being a baby-stealing demon (one of many). I didn't know about the rich mystical culture of protective magic that she brought with her, of amulets, incantation bowls, coded prayers, and strange angels, the birdlike Senoy and Sansenoy, and Semangelof, who looks like a Z with feet. I had none of that protection. But, being a Goth, I was wearing ornate, gaudy brass upside-down cross earrings intended to offend my father, who was easily offended by any reference to Christianity – for example by me, at eleven, singing along to the radio as it played Depeche Mode's 'Personal Jesus'.

The Devil, meanwhile, is waiting. How do I know they're the Devil? It's not the hat. This is Camden. Every era, fashion, fetish, vintage passes through these arches unremarked. It's not the whiskey – three fingers – in a tumbler when most people are drinking beers. It's not that I can't see their face in any detail, tilt of the brim, nor the fact I can hear the absolute grain of their voice although it's pitched low and soft, and the ABBA is loud. There is not a glitching neon bar sign pointing red at their head.

The Devil, finally, is given away by their fingernails, or rather, their cuticles, which do not exist. Their hand around the glass is like a moulded mannequin hand, the fingernails perfect in shape and angle but of the same material as the skin that surrounds them, although not coterminous with it. The nailbed is marked, but not by a cuticle. Not in the sense of holy shit, the perfect manicure, but in that obvious uncanny way that something is what it is and is not what it should be.

The Devil, they – meaning Christians – say, makes work for idle hands. The studied idleness of their smooth hands had obviously taken work. Their right hand gripped, lifted the glass (just in case you're thinking I'd been fooled by a mannequin), set it down, plucked a thread from their perfect left sleeve, all the while continuously speaking to me in that resonant quietness that exceeded all amplification to sound brass in my skull.

The Devil, alas, did not buy me a drink. Although I think they would have done if I'd said yes to their proposal. Which was?

All I had to do was say 'yes' and my father would be dead. Ease. Security. Instantaneous, invisible. Clean hands.

The Devil, besides. Beside me. I could tell you I was beside myself, but I wasn't. Not an out-of-body experience, although I'd had plenty of those. Ankles turning on my heels, Goth-thick tights itching, I considered it. Of course I did. I'd listened to my yetzer hara plenty, although often been too cowardly and lazy – those saving graces – to act. I'm a defender of water-cooler vengeance, a child of the OT God and of older Furies. But I did not say yes.

The Devil was, undoubtedly, and I had no doubts that if I said 'yes' something would happen. And it was that 'yes' that let in doubt. Something would happen, maybe not the next day, but one day, and I'd wonder (Carrie Bradshaw voice), *was it on me?* If that isn't just the late capitalist definition of agency. A few years later I'd drunkenly see a Midnight Madness screening of Virginie Despentes and Coralie Trinh Thi's *Baise-Moi*, a wild ride of a rape revenge film, and wonder. A project of projection, of sublimation into fiction, a fantasy with a hard realist edge that upset the easily unnerved cis male critic brigade, boo hoo. So, maybe I was supposed to write the story, that story, my story, verbal vengeance, pen mightier, etc. Maybe if I could stay alive long enough.

&

Is my father still alive? I don't know. And I don't care. It's taken some to get there. I can see now that what the Devil offered me would have been a life that, in its consequence, would never be unbound from my father. Call it a dead rather than living relationship to hell, end-stopped, stuck in the still, dark, atemporal zone of the dead. Yet here you are writing about him, again, you say. Devil's advocate.

What I saw in the neon instant, in that bar, was the difficulty of escape. And I chose it, chose to go not round but through. I threw some more booze at the issue, just to see if it would help. I went to more queer bars. I wore more gloriously impractical shoes. I fucked some impractically glorious people. None of these things solved the problem, except insofar as they kept me tethered to a sometimes-unbearable (insofar as it had him in it) world.

Things keep (us) going. There's a song – a drinking song, or rather a drunken song – sung fulsomely, with animal noises,

TRUTH & DARE

at the end of Passover Seder night. It's called 'Chad Gadya', 'One Goat', and it gives Wolf Mankowitz's novel, filmed by Carol Reed, its title: *A Kid for Two Farthings*. It's a cumulative song like 'There Was an Old Lady Who Swallowed a Fly', a song about consequences that, in a typical Ashkenazi *oy vey* way, escalates from buying a goat to the arrival of the Angel of Death in around three minutes. Maybe if you sell a kid for two bits you deserve all the malakh ha-mavet you get.

At the end of the song, the kid's still been sold. Time does not roll backwards, only relentlessly forwards in a drunken stumble. I did become a queer anarchivist of community spaces and conversations, ta-dah! The Black Cap Community Benefit Society has a business plan and is trying to strike a deal to buy the closed venue. Its activism inspired Friends of the Joiners Arms to keep alive a queer-run community space in Hackney. We save what we can, where we can. Parts of the story, fragments of the shimmer: first times and last times, strange angels and strangers we encounter. It's as easy to poeticise as it is to mark progress, and I don't know how this story – my story – ends.

It's hard to find a dismount that isn't a moral: the Devil knows that too. A price to pay for a price paid. This is how the Devil makes their story: not quite to your face, but close enough. Close enough to your ear. Close enough that you can feel their warmth and smell their smoke. Close enough for possibility. Close because you're listening.

House of Change

for Masha & Maya

The rabbi who performed a renaming ceremony at my apartment said that Jews believed the act of a name change could summon the Messiah.
— Ari M Brostoff, 'Exodus: Pekudai', *Jewish Currents*

He turned around, and saw to his astonishment that where before there had been a ruined house, he now stood in the yard of what seemed to be a prosperous, well-run farm. The door was open, and through it he could see a wide hearth where an orange fire burned low.
— Alison Croggon, *The Singing*

It's the collider's coming-out party. Array yourselves. It is Adar 4950, or what the English goyim call March 1190. See how time travels. It is already the future for some but not others. They've – we've – been busy that extra three and a half thousand years. Getting ready. The longest make-up session

TRUTH & DARE

in history. Every eyelash, every moustache, every tassel, every packer, every tattoo, every new name, every whatever makes you you, just a little bit more you.

The Jews of York are – have been – will have been going to be – building a particle collider powered by bread. And gender energy. Feeling it. All that glitter and vibration.

We've been planning this trip to the House of Change in York for *literally* ever. Opening day, finally. Because really, there's so much that needs to change. Us included.

&

What will we find there?

The door will open, and through it we will see a wide hearth where an orange fire burns low, awaiting. Of course it's the kitchen where the transformation happens. It's not shochet science. The Large Challah Collider. Bread-based fission. The realisation was pretty simple, really: yeast is alive. And kind of sexy. It buds, multiplies, if you feed it.

That is why there is no yeast in matzah: matzah is flat time, linear time, lived time, a reminder of what it's like to be trapped in dominant history. No bubbles, bubbeleh, no way to escape. Yeast begets yeast begets yeast begets bread begets both yeast and feast, and keeps going. In us. We are part of the cycle. Undeniable. Four-braided challah is superstring theory.

&

SO MAYER

If the Jews of York had not found their collider in kabbalah and challah, then we could not be here *or* there. Being there, we will not remember here, can only be there, which will be all our here. That is what it means to be present.

Of course, doubters say that the collider is, was, and will have been presaging, inadvertently – perhaps better to say preceding, as time's linearity is in fact the issue – death by a conflagration, an English pogrom written out of your history books.

Let us write it back in. It is 1190, the last Sabbath before the Jewish festival of Passover.

It's hard to write this in the cold objective manner of a tourist information board when it's about a massacre. It's hard to knead the dough of it when we have only the barest scraps of the recipe. But what survives matters. Even a few yeasty scraps. The day it happens, then, is the Sabbath before Passover. Holy enough that it's Shabbat, but Shabbat Hagadol is, literally, the big one. The deep breath before the memory of exile – but also, as they braided their challahs, the Jews of York might have been thinking that next week they would make matzot, and with matzah the baseless accusation of the blood libel rises, while matzah, made only of flour and water and not Christian children's blood, does not.

So it is Shabbat, time of contemplation and prayer, when the warning comes: the earls who have borrowed heavily to support the new king's crusading don't want to repay their debts. Or perhaps have been told not to. And so, leaving

TRUTH & DARE

aside blessing but taking togetherness, much of York's Jewish community, around 150 people, takes shelter in Clifford's Tower. It's a trap, and they are soon surrounded by an angry mob demanding that they be slaughtered or forcibly baptised. So, they kill themselves and burn the tower.

Do they, though? you ask. If you've never heard of it, did it even happen? And if it did, surely it was because of your, er, their dangerous experiments with being different? Things did not have to turn out that way, you say, if they'd just given in. Converted. And if they didn't have to turn out that way, you say, then surely it can be objectively said that they did not happen at all.

And you say our experiments with time are frightening.

&

We live after the fire, in the ruined yard.

But we do not yet remember the pogrom because we are, from the moment we enter the collider, in time. We will not be going to be able to remember what is about to always have been going to happen. Any more than their experiments, their inquisitiveness can cancel the Inquisition. But through them, to us, something did persist. It is how and why we-here-now (when and as we are, were and will again be in something called here-now, which is your future, when we are/were/will be outside this chamber) could build this transport in which we now – are? are not? – travelling towards that moment that is also now a here-now.

SO MAYER

All of us in time-diaspora are Messiahs, because messianic time is ... different. And yet the same. You experience it every day. In the heartbeats of, say, coming. Everything is so fucking beautiful. So fucking congruent, right? That feeling, that. Click. Christians say grace, from gratias, thanks. We'll take that. Being a messiah is no big deal, the daily deal, time on a two-for-one. It's what happens in exile, moving through time. We bring news. We bring ourselves. We arrive, and change happens.

We are changed. It's hard to describe our current state. Call it energy, in that it retains some spark of each entity who assented to this travel.

&

It's the *yes* of congruence and assent that turns out to be key. Transition, affirmation, play, naming and unnaming, celebration: gender euphoria releases big, whew. We spell out the rainbow that will arc beyond this moment: Richard overlords York's gender-bread in vain. The recipe will be handed down. As the great doctor Maimonides, blessed be his memory, wrote in his now-lost magnum opus, *The Guide for the Gender-Perplexed*:

> All bodies, made by God, know what and how they want to be. Let not the edicts of Pharaoh prevent you, for becoming yourself is a mitzvah. Take counsel with the learnèd at the House of Change in your city, who will share with you the knowledge of generations gone and

yet to come. To contribute, herein I include an account of the unguents I have learned, that you may prepare them, and the treatments developed and developing, that – should you wish them – you may prepare for them.

Breathe into your solar plexus, the knot of yourself where the divine lives. What does it tell you? Outbreath can begin a change of state, a realisation. Keep breathing. Breath may become speech, may become act, maybe become community [synagogus].

Rabbi Yomtov, a noted scholar, comes in the late twelfth century to York from Joigny in France, bearing manuscripts in Arabic and Hebrew that have crossed the border from Al-Andalus. Metaphysics, a mathematics of realising the divine. Medical treatises infused with song lyrics, dance steps, and recipes. This is healing.

The Rabbi, whose name means Good day, or Holy day, will greet us with words from a manuscript that has just been delivered to him, rushed from Córdoba, a book that changes the world: Ibn Rushd's *Kitab fasl al-maqal*, or *On the Harmony of Religions and Philosophy*. Non-binary finery from the great polymath, champion of our shared intellection, who identified the retina, a sensitivity to light that few could perceive. Rabbi Yomtov recites Ibn Rushd's yearning words:

> There is a sense of loneliness: the philosophers are called weeds [nawābit], like the grass that springs up among the crops; they are strangers in their own country.

SO MAYER

Don't let us be lonely, but be weeds together. We are ready.

&

And the world – 1190 version – needs it. In Westminster before the palace, they are flying the Cross of St George as the English flag for the first time. Cynical manoeuvre to steal the Genoese flag as a non-fungible token for free movement in the Mediterranean (no return). Look what's coming home.

The House of Change knows the age of the Crusades, precursor to empire, is coming. Before translocation (geographical and temporal), they had divination. It is like this: particles are entangled. If we are coming, we were always going to have been coming, with all our knowledge. Absorbing it, however, isn't instant. Time takes time. Great libraries of future to read through, as you do with your libraries of the past. Moments of happenstance still have to happen; you have to experience recognition, encounter, emergence.

Here we are.

&

Although there is a moment where   here   we
&   are   fall away.

Instead, there are four of us, and I mean four of *us*. As in, iterations, from across the time diaspora. Four identical yet wildly different possibilities of us. Why four? It's a metonym for many more, a calling of the corners. One with a key, one with a knife, one with a mirror, one with hands flat on the table. There is no table. There is no there there.

Centuries later/ago, a Ukrainian Jewish American filmmaker who can see through the illusion of history will place this image in a film so that we have a visual metaphor to share with you. Gracias, Maya – or Mayas, there being, by a trick of editing, four of you on screen – for *Meshes of the Afternoon*, made as war was overtaking you in California in 1942.

&

We get there and the house is hidden – or, rather, different. It takes a slant of eye to see it. From the outside, it appears to be a gatehouse, a tower. A protection spell because nowhere is safe.

Inside the bailiwick, the stone walls melt away and we realise that what we saw was, as it must have been, a single-storey wooden house, a schoolhouse of the northern lands, built of planed timber. The joints still smell of pitch in the summer, or when something's cooking, as it is now.

Ima Chaim is resplendent in tallith and velvet skirt at the hearth, her challah thrust into the embers, their tzimmes in the cauldron, stirring, stirring. Small bright suns of carrot glazed in citrus and honey, the sign of this day. We make our greetings and leave him in the sweet-scented steam that is building, the air scintillant with spices rising from copper bowls whose tones ghost the high ceiling.

A swagged tabby cat darts past, moth in its mouth, and we follow it into a small library of manuscripts and parchments and tablets, where we leave our offering alongside paperbacks and data crystals and scrolls and broadsides and quipu and quilts and zines. The cat darts up the half-flight of stairs to a beamed attic where people are dancing in the silence of bodies, breath and steps and laughter and, yes, collisions. Channelling energy to the hearth heating below them.

We watch, breathing with them, until the door besides us opens out onto a ridged field rich in rocks and moss, backed by a shed full of implements and spare parts, from ropes and horseshoes and long-handled wooden ladles to bolts of silvery fabrics and breastforms, all you could need. The cat sits, tail curled into a this-way sign, by a stack of wooden buckets. We take one and follow the outcurve of the tail to the ritual bath, the mikveh, where we immerse ourselves in fresh spring water into which we can never step twice, yet it is full of every person who has passed, is passing, or will pass through this caravanserai between worlds.

Through an arch in the bath house, we reach the next stage of transformation. The steam bath: the hammam, whose tiles express the mysteries of how we fit together, of how repetition engenders transformation, how we tesselate from small decisions into bigger patterns, dancing the cosmos of ourselves.

This is healing, in the silence of bodies sighing out, shifting, sweating. Hearts beating. In the rising heat, with

TRUTH & DARE

each breath, we share our scars, our marks and alterations. Inhale OKness, acceptance, the fine spray of sublimation, water into steam. Yes. Everything is changing.

&

When we step out into the spring freshness, into fresh robes of hemp or silk or nothing, we see what is written on this side of the House of Change, in twigs that make the shape of the Hebrew letters: Yom Tov to the spirit of awakening.

The poet John Donne will later reduce it to: Good-morrow to our waking souls, making a real mess even as he reaches for that yes. As he will of: Bread batter is the heart, four-braided, of the Divine in us (Batter my heart, three-person'd God? Oh, John. Cis men really will write poetry rather than go to therapy), which sings forth from the tapestry hanging on the kitchen wall. Literally sings: weaving is music, the thread of the universe in all its colours and spheres, in a form Reb Yomtov brought in his throat over the ocean from Córdoba.

> And the muwashshaḥāt, if we listen to them, help us hear and see a medieval Europe crafted out of that most intimate of dances with the other – an other who lives very much within our house ... [The songs] invent new Romance and Arabic and Hebrew poetics in one swoop, all in the same poem ... a calliope of languages and voices.

SO MAYER

So it will be written, be writing, and has been written, in María Rosa Menocal's *Shards of Love: Exile and the Origins of the Lyric*. We think of the book, and it appears on the kitchen window seat, well thumbed for its invocations of this very moment, of what could have been.

&

The fire has reached its shimmer. Everywhere, laughter; tender. The slow reveal of skin, of curves that have been dreamed, of marks that have been chosen, healing. Please, touch, gently. The stipple and ruche, the remnant heat, the fullness. Child of blessèd deed: ba* mitzvah. A coming of ages, time taken into the flesh and released. Here, now.

The truth is: trans *is* Jewish, inclusive. God is non-binary as angels are, messengers in the ancient world being the gender of their sender, and God's being whatever they want to be. What it means to be in a body, differently, is what the Crusades take aim against. Repeatedly, locked into linear time, always fighting for the straight line. But we keep going. Our yeasts, metonymically. Give ourselves a little sugar and bloom. The truth is: we do. Ferment. Cause it. Fermi, Fermat, fermentation. It's all bubbling and rising, ourselves the altar of our selves. Not sacrifice but gift. This time. This time. We will.

We come together. There is nothing linear about our desire. Legs entwined like challah braids, if you like. Soft sighs tuned to the embroidery, and to the sweet bite of caramelised roots. Sprawl, fall to your knees. Be open, as the universe is. As the collider is.

&

We walk. To the beat, to the cheers. York is burning.

And then, York is burning.

Power never hesitates. What it senses as resistance is just us, being. What it calls violence, its own actions projected and deflected. They come bearing the blood libel: that we are harming children. That we are secret paedophiles, when it is they who lock children in monasteries, rape them in churches, work them in mines, send them to die in Crusades. They state their crime by writing it in our name.

They will steal the words of us, even. Domus Conversorum will be built in London, in Chancery Lane: House of the Changed, meaning converted, where a chosen few conversos will be allowed to do business that benefits the Commonwealth. A wall to exclude us, a ghetto where we will, in secret, crypto, hidden, do what they least expect. Rebuild. Reclaim.

What challah reminds us: nothing is a closed loop. This burns, that we cannot escape. The tower falls in flames, even as the very eye of time comes open. They will call it suicide. Sometimes the only choice is between stealth, death, or exile, that trinity of three-in-one, same difference. Nothing to disapprove, no win or lose: there is no right move. We do we.

&

SO MAYER

The thing that burns is the circle. Every time. Every loss. Each repetition.

But it is not recursive. We refuse that logic. Nor is it progress. What matters is the coming together, that's what the collider knows. Each instance of connection, each impression on the other, each exchange: that is forever. The difference between infinity and eternity is *that* forever, always expanding, always rippling outwards in possibility. Yeast begets yeast begets yeast begets bread begets both yeast and feast. We are part of the cycle. Undeniable.

But so is the grief. To land here, again, with empty hands, hands empty but for burned skin. How could this smell be pleasing to the Lord? It is not the warm earth smell of baking bread, nor the salt-sweet smell of sunskin. Not the smoke sting of warming fire on a cold night. And yet it has its share in all of them, that's the bitter choke in the throat. Flesh is flesh. We burn, just like all living things. We burn because we are living things, carbon and fat and, oh, oxygen.

Gasp it in. The chamber is nautilus-curved like the inside of a shofar, a great winding rise that offers us a soft landing in its lowest bay. Its shape is something to do with time, something to do with resuscitation. It draws air in from the narrowest point of its chimney far above us, and spirals it down to us where we half-float, as if on tears.

This is hard. Hard to believe in change when it is not universal, permanent; to hold faith to the local transformation, the moment with its unpredictable effects. It is hard

TRUTH & DARE

not to feel that this is a noose caught around us, a gone last chance. To feel looped and unsteady with it.

But if time is linear, all you do is grieve. History is not fixed. We hold to that. Even so – and because – the forces of stasis, the quo of the status, are not only powerful and resourceful, overwhelming in number, but also ruthless. They will stop at nothing.

And so, we keep having to return to this moment, which is nothing, this absence in which we have consented to place our selves for the sake of. Time does not need us, but we like to feel it as need, and so transform ourselves over and again. To be nothing, in the space between. We will keep going. We will keep believing. Breathing. Deep breath.

A knife. A key. A mirror. Hands on the table. One step, then another. Distance no distance.

We come back to ourselves.

There are more of us.

Every time, more.

Changing =>

The water molecule is so common that it is wise to just memorise that water is a *bent* molecule.

Underwater, you have no breast tissue.

No wide hips, no soft pouch of belly, no wobbling arse or dappled thighs.

Underwater, the fat of you persists, but sleeked into hydrodynamic ripples of blubber wrapped in navy-blue-almost-black-with-moisture lycra. Is it the reflection of light patterns shifting on the bottom of the pool, or has the water contorted you?

It could be the lower gravity, or it could be the bent molecules, where the two lone electron pairs (invisible when looking at molecular geometry) exert a little extra repulsion on the two bonding hydrogen atoms to create a slight compression to a 104° bond angle.

When you are swimming, you know what this means, in your mucosal membranes, in your 73% water lungs, in your 79% water muscles.

You use an app called Otter to transcribe what your voice

makes, what others' voices make. You don't understand the code that drives the AI behind it, or why you always tick yes, the AI can use your corrected transcript to improve itself. You like to be helpful. You like to be part of something. You imagine it – the app, or the data it processes; no, the interface behind and within them – as both the swimmer and the pool, the invisible bonds behind the molecular geometry of natural language. It cannot understand names, abbreviations, slang. Your conversations become formal, spelled out. The singularity is here. You serve the machine. You serve it because it means you do not have to listen back to your voice in order to transcribe. It removes you from you, making a language-you that is all surface, in which you can hear the depths that resonate when bent by the bone echo chamber of your skull but are not caught on tape. You'd rather be the machine, or product thereof.

The pool is not a machine, yet it is. Metaphorically. An interface, a bluescreen, data. You enter into it. Enter your pheromones and skin cells to be processed by the chlorine. It's not literal, is it? You do not wear a Fitbit or whatever. But you book online, because you have to, and pay with a traceable digital source. You swipe your card through the turnstile. You fill in the leisure-centre survey. You like to be helpful. You like to prove you are more than how your body is perceived by others, including yourself. You know you are being seen. The pool is monitored. The sky is monitored. You check the helicopters that pass overhead. You use your phone to check the humidity, the pollen count, the pollution.

SO MAYER

Refraction occurs at the water–air boundary.

As you turn at the end of the lane, gasping in dirty air because the pool is beside a main road, you go Möbius, a Mandelbrot infraction. There is visual distortion, and it is not the water beading at the silicon seal of your goggles, worn so tight you have goggling octopus eyes.

As above, so below: you refract at the water–air boundary just as sound does.

Head up, you can hear the displaced school-gate chatter between the parents accompanying the primary school splash class, buses lumbering on the main road, the post-menopausal comparisons of the two skirted bathers lounging at the end of the lane, drains and filters and lockers clanging, the Saturday-night gossip between the lifeguards, the climate change mansplaining of the expensively tattooed Speedos cruising towards you.

Underwater, nothing. Just the pressure of your own breath, a hum in it as you expel too fast and come up spluttering before the end of the lane as a small child jumps in suddenly, right there in front of you. Say sorry to the lady, says an adult. It would be as churlish to say, I'm not a lady, as to say that after twelve is lane swimming; you should use the paddling pool. Both are true; neither is socially acceptable.

Above the waterline is the body you move around in every day, with its partially functional lungs, its hip dysplasia, and arthritic left foot with three badly healed breaks – you could go on, from top to toe, elaborating every slight and failing, a list syncopated to the asthmatic arrhythmia of your breathing.

Below the waterline you are none of these things, have none of them. Your underwater body is buoyant and pain-free. What feet? All muscle is just muscle. The bubble of your breath is not heaving and uneven, but a song.

A list of all the injuries you've sustained while immersed:

- chipped and cracked front teeth
- concussion
- two broken toes
- a broken finger
- ear infections
- skin infections
- infected piercings
- a ripped-off toenail
- giardiasis
- sunburnt armpits
- asthma attacks
- a split lip from being kicked in the face
- torn muscles
- a dislocated hip
- a knee gashed on rocks
- ass-grabbing
- humiliation.

In fairness, you've sustained many similar injuries – excepting giardiasis, although it repeats – when on dry land.

But the question stands: why keep throwing yourself into deep water – and not just metaphorically.

One time, you were pulled out by a lifeguard. You had stopped breathing, partly of your own volition, although it didn't feel wilful. You'd blanked out before you'd blacked out, lost concentration. Forgot you were in a medium where respiration demands attention, intention. It was the second time that your swimming life came to an end. More from fear of further humiliation than of death. How *inconvenient* you felt, how forcefully re-embodied in all your meaty sprawlingness.

To be hauled. To be borne. To be *saved*.

To end up in the wrong body, the one that is hauled and borne by others, including you. Stupid chlorine tears in your eyes refract the ceiling lights and you see that other underwater body, shimmering. Starfishing, its lung capacity infinite. Out of reach. You have been signed out of the screen.

The underwater body winks out of existence as you dash the tears and snot from your face, telling the guard that you're fine. Slipping (literally) into the changing room before anyone can call an ambulance. The balance is tipped: you are refracted. You leave without your underwater body as if it were the sports centre towel you paid two quid for and have to return on your way out. Flinging it into the overflowing bin. Another damp cast-off, worn-through cotton with PROPERTY OF —— ironed on to the corner. It will be several years before you remember the password.

TRUTH & DARE

Recent research reveals that the water found on most comets and asteroids contains on average more deuterium – itself a hydrogen isotope – than water on Earth, suggesting that our water might date back to the origin of the solar system. Remaining below the surface may have prevented it from evaporating during the early years of planetary formation. Rocks 1000 kilometres deep can store water.

There is a muscle memory of the first time you stopped swimming.

Your age-thirteen double Ds are too heavy for the standard-issue school high-V, low-back Speedo, in the long years before underwired swimwear or binders. You're shamed in the changing room for your body hair, its werewolf excess compared with that of the other early adolescents in your year. You are pubescing, pubes-ing, faster than they are. Darker than they are. Wiry and unwaxed. Your mother forbids hair removal, mourning her own plucked-out eyebrows. It's not exactly *King Lear*, as tragedies go.

You learn about Effie Ruskin. You learn about feminism. You see Patti Smith on the cover of *Easter*. You find queer zines in record stores. You think it will get easier.

These days you get shouted at in a changing room for having unshaven legs, and handed a disposable razor. Then you get shouted at for shaving your legs in the shower. You get shouted at for wearing board shorts and a rash vest instead of the expected bikini. You get shouted at for splash-kicking the swimmer grabbing your ass in the water. You get shouted at, your bag thrown at you, for being at the Ladies' Pond.

You read that the brain uses water to manufacture hormones and neurotransmitters. You don't know whether to drink more or hold your breath until it all goes away. The body that is seen above the waterline, the body on the sidelines. Your password is all wrong. You cannot enter. The underwater body is a non-fungible token you cannot afford and do not believe in anyway.

You are the injury. You are a visual distortion, an infection. Your leg hair could clog the drains not only of this pool but of the whole borough. You are a slow monster.

> An aquatic system lacking dissolved oxygen (0% saturation) is termed anaerobic, reducing, or anoxic; a system with low concentration – in the range between 1% and 30% saturation – is called hypoxic or dysoxic. Most fish cannot live below 30% saturation, since oxygen is required to derive energy from nutrients. Hypoxia leads to impaired reproduction of remaining fish via endocrine disruption [lacking citation].

Some things never change: the echoeyness that persists, transferred from the waterlogged space of the pool and changing rooms to your waterlogged ear, the astonishingly hot sting of urine as you slide against the toilet seat on cold, wet thighs for that first post-swim piss. A kind of violence ripping through your muscles under the shower: the desire to be alone, to be alone with your body, to be in your body, this body in its brief moment of still being that body.

Sometimes you want to piss in the shower. There's a drain right there. Sometimes you look at the black mould on the ceiling and your skin crawls. Sometimes towards it. Sometimes there's a wave of arousal that is uncontainable by clinging wet chlorinated board shorts. It burns hotter than the shower water, even when the settings are broken and set to blanch. In the next cubicle, a small child is screaming 'Mashed potato mashed potato mashed potato'.

That must be what you want. You stop at the supermarket on the way home, and buy five things, none of which are potatoes. None of which are the answer.

Right out of the pool, there is the craving for food that cancels out the chlorine – throughout your childhood, pickled onion Monster Munch was the ritual offering. Now, wise to the monosodium glutamate and disodium 5'-ribonucleotide, to the nose-curl of whey permeate, you settle for a snack bar, pretending it really tastes like chocolate and not pre-masticated dates. Pretending it is food and not fancy Soylent Green.

What's good for you: regular swimming, fruit, phthalate-free shower gel, regulating your mobile-phone use, getting off social media, getting off the sofa. Don't think of yourself as pollution. Don't google it. Don't follow that Reddit thread. Don't obsess. Don't plan your life around it. Don't drown in it. Nod that you are hypoxic and need to breathe more. Don't question that you are impaired, that impaired is the word. That this is disruption, that you lack citation. Don't question the contradiction.

Smile more. Laugh more. Stretch more. Be the person with the most fish. Try not to swallow the pool water. Try not to swear in your head at the guy swimming behind you who keeps 'accidentally' grabbing your ankle, your knee, your butt. Try not to stop breathing. Let it not make sense, even just for the second you are moving through it.

> The Mpemba effect describes the observation that hot water will freeze faster than cold water under certain conditions. In 1963, Tanzanian student Erasto Bartholomeo Mpemba observed this while making ice cream, having accidentally skipped a cooling stage. In 1969, he co-authored a paper analysing the phenomenon, entitled 'Cool?'

Your friend J tells you about swimming in the bubbles of the swimmer in front of you. Slipstreaming. That sounds cool, you say. But the thought is hot on your skin, the weird hot of those tiny corporate hotel pools you've snuck into. Something sticky about it, the kind of sticky that is the sign of something unlocking. It is as simple as if you have skipped a cooling stage. You have never been cool, always hot, hot with shame. You jump into the water and ask its search engine, What does it feel like to be in a body that is just a body – an abode, an entity?

It is a child body at elemental play when you tell yourself

TRUTH & DARE

you should be working, an animal body with fur and fear, fight or flight rising up over your usual freeze. Can't freeze in the water. A body that ripples with those arabesques of light that rise up from the gritty floor of the pool.

If light is a wave as well as a particle. If light speed is a measure of both space and time. Your body ripples with time, with times: all the times it has been immersed and moving, all the times it has been becoming, molecular patternings. Your underwater body that could be – has always been – yours.

Slipstream.

oestro junkie

There was the time I had an alien baby.

Complete with invasive examinations and memory loss, and nothing to show for it but this.

&

Sometimes it takes an alien abduction to learn about your own body. It shouldn't have to, but. It shouldn't be this hard, either. GCSE biology both lied to me, and bored me – drove me away, in a handshake with female socialisation, from my ambition to be a forensic pathologist (and this was before *The X-Files*). Sometimes, as Dana Scully knows, it takes an alien abduction to show you you're being lied to.

The alien wasn't an alien, and the abduction wasn't an abduction, but. A burst ovarian cyst I didn't know I had. A Friday night A&E doctor who is trained to assume it was an ectopic pregnancy, to assume it was an STI, to assume consent. It hurt.

Trained to assume, as a medical student friend later told me, that 'all girls are liars because their hormones make them crazy'.

TRUTH & DARE

&

Gina Rippon notes that the 'so-called female hormone[s] ... were named oestrogens, from the Greek terms oistrus (mad desire) and gennan (to produce). (You can probably guess the gender of the scientists who named them thus.)'

The *OED* has the full scoop, as always:

> classical Latin oestrus gadfly, wild desire, frenzy < ancient Greek οἶστρος [oistros] gadfly, insect that infects tunny fish, also sting, hence frenzy, mad impulse (< the same Indo-European base as Lithuanian aistra violent passion) < the same base as οἷμα [oima] impulse, attack, rage, probably cognate with Avestan aēšma- anger, classical Latin īra

Irate, indeed. But what are you meant to do when the effect is ... actual? Here's the thing: my mindbody is allergic to my own oestrogen. That's the simplest way to say it, what scientists have finally got around to acknowledging as premenstrual dysphoric disorder, only recently isolated and named something other than 'bad' premenstrual syndrome or symptoms, which themselves remain barely credited by the medical establishment.

The working hypothesis concerns oestrogen's effect on serotonin. Or possibly an oestrogen–progesterone imbalance that ... brain farts? Or possibly something to do with anxiety. Or, you know, something. Shrug. Have some SSRIs and be quiet.

SO MAYER

What if the rage, the frenzy, comes from being denied the tools to understand yourself, let alone heal yourself?

&

Of late, testosterone has developed a bit of a bibliography, even if it's a lit review of how little we actually know: Katrina Karkazis and Rebecca M Jordan-Young's heavyweight *Testosterone: An Unauthorized Biography* delves into the biochemical complexity of testosterone and its uptake, and demonstrates that previous studies linking the hormone to violence and sporting prowess did no such thing, just stirred a cocktail of racism and classism into sexism and brewed. Cordelia Fine's psychological survey *Testosterone Rex* treats the studies as legit, which is annoying, but still shows that T is not the king of anything other than false assumptions to shore up cisheteropatriarchy's fragility. And, of course, there's Paul B Preciado's wild autotheoretical *Testo Junkie*. That's a lot of T, in a timely fashion, and all fascinating. Thrilling, even, and brilliant.

Yet, despite the use of oestrogens in transition, fertility treatment, post-menopausal therapies, contraception, the treatment of schizophrenia, and for extremely dubious, ableist, or homophobic 'purposes', such as growth attenuation and to discipline and punish men convicted of having sex with men, like Alan Turing, there are no cultural, historical, psychological, neurological, or autotheoretical studies that I know of – although there are plenty of conflicting and contradictory self-help books about HRT, along with shit-tonnes of exhortatory diet books. Are they all pink? Yes, of course. I do not rate.

&

Maybe that's because science and 'mad desire' just aren't compatible? Or rather, not science but its cultural history and theory. Because it's a truth universally acknowledged that anything associated with AFAB, female, feminine, or femme mindbodies, in all their constellations, must a priori be ahistorical and acultural.

&

Less acknowledged, including by me, is that I am a science nerd. I wasn't much like the skilled protagonists of *Rosie Revere, Engineer* or *Izzy Gizmo*, or the other new picture book characters whom I love to bits, who are inventors, tinkerers, and aviation enthusiasts. What excited me was higher maths (so-called 'pure maths') and theoretical physics, and their cultural histories. They still excite me, but I didn't have the determination to pursue my interests to path-breaking achievement.

Science nerd was a pretty dead-end street in my upbringing. Applied maths was useful for household accounting; even the Jewish book of prayer acknowledges that, in the song known in English as 'A Price Above Rubies'. But in terms of both gender assignment and class, there was no possible route I could follow that led through maths, higher maths, physics and … The sky was limited.

I détourned my passion into a love of feminist science fiction, which has constantly broadened my horizons, fed my appetite for complexity, and led me to question the foundations of Eurowestern science and its myths about itself. And it was in fact via *The X-Files* (long story short) that I encountered the work of feminist science thinkers like Donna Haraway, Anne Fausto-Sterling, Evelyn Fox Keller, Sandy Stone, Anne Balsamo, and more.

My personal history and theory of science and technology has been profoundly linked to embodiment and to labour, but Haraway's cyborg is a reminder that the human body is no longer a pure entity, if it ever was: hybrid with and by natureculture, it is a cyborg. Embodiment is also technological, and vice versa. And that matters. It defines what it means to be matter, material. How I'm coming to matter to myself, moreover.

&

It's not the evidenced biochemical basis of premenstrual dysphoric disorder that made it 'real' to me: it's that I began to research it only after I presented myself as gender non-aligned and began to sort through the ways I felt (bad) in and about my body, realising that some were constant and some cyclical. It was the first step towards being what Haraway calls a relational scientist, someone who places themselves in their experimental practice as it emerges from their own embodied experience in community.

Reconnecting to history and theory of science from feminist, queer, trans, critical race, and disability perspectives makes me realise we are *all* scientists, but neither in a purist sense of lab coats, goggles, and arguments for depoliticised objectivity nor in a sense that evacuates the many, multiple, transhistorical practices of science.

Let's say that the rigorous observation of phenomena at all scales should be available to all, as should the attempt not only to understand them but to narrate them comprehensibly in relation to the observer, often with experiments to affect said phenomena through equally rigorously observed and fully narrated interventions. It would mean thinking differently about what we call 'child's play' and what we call magic or primitive belief systems – but also about what we call science, a lot of which is neither rigorous nor comprehensible, and whose interventions are often motivated by politics, economics, and prejudice.

&

Or, my mother was a computer.

When I read that sentence in Balsamo's *Technologies of the Gendered Body*, I laughed out loud at its boldness. All the stuff I'd been learning about the difference engine clicked into place. Oh, of course: not *that* kind of story, all clacking and

SO MAYER

cliffhangers and bodies *without* organs, but this messy, fleshy thing that does work, however it can (get paid).

Balsamo goes on to explain that 'computer' was a term for early programmers in the US, most of whom were women, as it was seen as secretarial work. But the striking image stayed with me. I think of Celeste (Colette Laffont) in Sally Potter's Marxist, feminist, anti-imperialist musical *The Gold Diggers*, realising that she is moving money she cannot access through her body: her Black butch body that is ignored and invisibilised in and by her job as a financial services worker in London. She hammers on the keys of her 1980s data-entry terminal, but nothing happens – except inside her mindbody, as she begins an investigation into capital that leads to her denouncing imperialism and resource extraction, and riding off on a white horse with Ruby (Julie Christie): what a promise.

It starts with her hands on the keys, with her deep understanding of living as part of a circuit. Being a computer, part of the matrix, awakens her.

Matrix: it's too overdetermined. Is related to mater; mother. My (other)mother *was* a computer, or at least, for some time, a wired-up incubator. How very *Matrix*. Except.

I find the idea of my othermother comforting rather than (Dr) Frankensteinian. Maybe that makes me a monster, and I'm OK with that. I find it comforting that my gestational mother didn't have to do all the work alone, that she had support and assistance from somewhere that was never going to come from my father.

TRUTH & DARE

At the bottom of this – let's be Freudian and call it the knotted navel, because my cyborg body had both kinds of cord, electrical and umbilical, attaching it to the world, and that makes me feel that attachment is beautiful – is the fantasy of a cyborgic conception taking place (only) between my gestational mother and the incubator. They conceived me, and – spooky action at a distance – they raised me.

&

In her beautiful study of the queer quantum life of scholarship *Haunted Data*, Lisa Blackman talks about how many things that are assumed to be biological, neurological, and even physical are 'culture all the way down'. It's a mind-blowing phrase, and a beautiful takedown of evolutionary biology, especially evolutionary psychology, as a bedtime story for scared little white boys who need a 'once upon a time' to give them the security of a 'patriarchally ever after'.

Which is not centrally the point, but it is. Origin myths are often deployed as narcissistic defences – but they don't have to be. Elsewhere in the book, Blackman pursues her main argument that, if we take quantum theory seriously, we have to believe that the future can change the past. Shortly after *Haunted Data* was published, it was announced that scientists working on an IBM quantum computer had, indeed, reversed time, something that's already known in the haunted – that is, queer – temporal displacements and play that Blackman discusses in her book.

SO MAYER

What I mean is: it's not science fiction to say we can rewrite our origin myths, personally and culturally, and rewrite them *away* from purism, exceptionalism, and hierarchies of value. It's not just lifelong brain plasticity that makes this possible. I don't just mean that we can change our minds and behaviours, which we can, but that we can travel back and change, if we need to, ab initio, ad infinitum, looping the open loop of the o of ourselves.

Lyonesses

Ma Morvoren y'n Benbow
Deun alemma, voyd alemma
An tekka yw yn oll Kernow
Kelmys on Ostrali.

There's a mermaid in the Benbow
Let's go, let's get away
The most beautiful in all of Cornwall
We're bound for Australia.
— 'Deun Alemma'

Mermaids, eh? You'll be wanting the Barbie Panini sticker album, not the FIFA one, they told us. And now here we are not just buying the stickers but appearing on them, all numbered shirts and crossed arms. They'd never believe it. Told us we'd never have the legs for it. That we'd be all over the pitch, hair getting in our faces, distracted by the dazzle and glare of the cameras and the fans, always trailing the opposition with tails between the sticks. Water carriers at best. And were we really women anyway?

We didn't listen. Stopped our ears with shoes, and ships, and sealing wax – except to the words of our coach, Dory.

Just keep swimming. Just keep swimming.

Ma Morvoren y'n Benbow.

And sing. Sing when you're winning. We knew we could be irresistible.

&

We're not going to lie: sometimes it is like running on hot knives.

We've come late to legs, to this division between them, so the timing of a tackle can throw us. Splashdown! Astroturf so much less forgiving than the ocean. Sometimes you just want the ground to swallow you up, but it doesn't, does it? It has no gulp, just bladed roughness. We all sport grazes, compare grass cuts in the bath afterwards. The pattern that gravel makes on a knee is not unlike scales. We touch the tiny depressions, pour salt on the small wounds, feel grainy, like we're breaking up. Get up and do it all again. Get knocked down and we get up again.

Just keep swimming, etc.

Don't call us divers, though. We know our opponents see us as easy targets, want to hack our legs from under us. Call them fake, then talk up our unfair advantage. Our unnatural body shape. Talk about cynical. But on the pitch, we bite our tongues, although then they call us dumb. Taunt us to sing, then, when *they* fall, call it cheating. When we fall, we stretch out each other's limbs, press them into the hum deep in our stomachs. We know where the cramp cramps in the new unfluid muscles as they try to swish and kink, powering us through sweaty air, around bodies as if coral.

Flick-on. It's on. We are still finding our feet, which gravity helps with. Anchoring, pointing This Way Up. Up and over, sometimes. We specialise in the bicycle kick, the flying finish. Our sweeper-keeper whose legs seem to move as one. The ball floating on the air like seafoam.

&

At exceptionally low spring tide, you can walk between the Scilly Isles. You can; we can. You even call the sound between St Mary's and Tresco 'The Road'.

Lyonesse, the city on the bottom of the sea, has always been amphibious – both and everything else, too. Bedrock and birdrock and tombolo, outcroppings of the Cornubian batholith. Deep rock nearly three hundred million years old, so the stories go, told from seawitch to seawitch of the Great Uprising, aka what you call the Variscan orogeny: magma making mountains in the seams of Pangaea's coming-together. Stretching from Galicia to the Bohemian massif and down into Turkey, pivoted on Montblanc, it's the fold belt that holds Europe together, a stone spine mirrored across the Mediterranean by the Anti-Atlas and across the Atlantic by the Appalachians.

TRUTH & DARE

Deun alemma, voyd alemma.

To use your words, which we hear in the deep. Water is a transmitter, a medium of echoes and resonances. Your radar that causes cetaceans to go off course, tortured by songs they can't respond to; singers calling to them of nowhere, out of nowhere. You have become what you fear of us, the fatal voice luring the world onto the rocks. Rocks you give names to, names that hiss and sizzle in our sea-ears, rocks you do not understand. We have grown on them like barnacles, grown with them. The seawitches say we too, in our first forms, swam forth as the Earth's crust extended, carried in the tides of granitic magma.

Hot knives, cooled to 1000°C. Fractures form along vertical joints. It is all one to us, and of us: under and over, hidden and exposed. Where we rub along the waves, where we come to the surface. Either way, we erode. Those fantastic shapes you call tors are our stopped bodies playing keepy-uppy, scattered about with the irreducible core of us, rounded and hard, to be navigated with care. What you call clitter is bearded with ferns and lichens, mossy and fox-holed, boulders all clustered and jumbled together, warm beneath you on a summer's day. Over here the clitter of Lustleigh Cleave, just below Harton Chest.

Be still my.

What we mean is: this land is us, magma-veined and weighty, cool enough to stand tall even if we crack slowly under pressure. We are the foot of the country dipped in between the English Channel and the Celtic Sea, toe pointed balletically, Ireland flying off our laces into the Atlantic's wide-open net. GOAAAALLLLLL.

How could we miss?

&

St Blazey AFC, across the river from Par, was the first place we walked onto pitch. Maybe the team's name made us think of those undersea fires that forged us, or it was the draw of Lostwithiel that called to us, sang of the lost city beneath the waves. Maybe it was just the club's gas-heated showers. The Par River runs alongside the pitch, down to St Austell Bay. We came around the Lizard heading northeast, ears ringing with the busy shipping lanes going south from Plymouth. Up into Carlyon Bay. Car-Lyon. Here we are, already. Sealions on our shirts. Here we go, here we go, here we go.

An tekka yw yn oll Kernow.

Summer of 2019, mostly cool and wet, like us. Late, late June aglitter all of a sudden and we're drawn up like a tide by the sounds of it, #FIFAWWC, the talk of the beaches and boats, the news of it crackling through submarine cables running from Sennen Cove and Porthcurno, Bude and Skewjack, across the Atlantic in thick skeins ablaze with the chatter. It had pricked our ears for the first time in 2015, voices going back and forth across the ocean, rising data usage, viewing figures, intensities. Four years on and it's coming home coming home; so-called. Not to Kernow, there's no Cornubians among the Lionesses. Bring back my bonny to me.

TRUTH & DARE

We made our fantasy first XI: our queen and hero Pinoe, who tells the press, 'You can't win without gay players,' playing for pride; seagreen-haired Gaëlle Enganamouit; Marta of the flaming lips; Wendie Renard rising above every challenge; Vanina Correa keeping the Albiceleste shining; Kadeisha Buchanan, magical youngest of seven sisters; Kim Little, the legend of Mintlaw; Yuka Momiki, who wrote her thesis on the women's game; *@rasheedatt10* sharing the Super Falcons' R&R on Insta; Lucy Bronze moving fluid as hot metal, strong as a statue. Phew. We argued their stats and their merits as we practised. We were – we are – all muscle. We are one long curving kick, used to the rough-and-tumble of the world's worsening weather. Used to being fished for, but getting something *into* a net, that we had to get used to.

Up until that day we sauntered up the Par in our glittering kits, stitched blue-green out of algae, St Blazey had never had a women's team. Despite being one of the oldest clubs in the county (founded 1896), they had no place in the Electrical Earthbound Cornwall Women's Football League. We must have seemed an unlikely fit, being neither eels nor, exactly, earthbound. But at level seven (seabed, bedrock, bottom feeders) who's to argue? Helston, Charlestown, Penryn, Illogan, Mousehole, Bude, FXSU, RNAS Culdrose, Newquay Celtic, Porthleven, and Wadebridge all fell before us in the 2019/20 season, and so too did the other saints (Agnes, whose hair grew and covered her body; Breward, bishop of Jersey; Teath, daughter of Brycheiniog and companion of Breaca), and lo! we were promoted to the South West Women's Football League

SO MAYER

Division One (West). To the South West Premier League. The FA Women's National League South, the Championship, the Women's Super League. Sing and keep singing.

Having climbed out of the sea, we kept climbing. Cliffs of fall and get up again. Just keep swimming. We split our training between exposed rock and our secret grounds undersea. Did high-intensity training in the photosynthesis chamber at the Eden Project, swimming high as kites in plant-exhaled oxygen behind the glass. Stashed our selkie skins in the club dressing rooms, kept moist by those gas-heated showers. Down the river and into the salt, our metamorphic world. Under pressure.

&

We swam to and from Women's Super League games as much as we could; swam round the south coast, risking all those shipping lanes and daytripping ferries, to meet Bristol, then on to Brighton & Hove, where we shimmied up the pier and cawed back at the seagulls to celebrate our 3–0 victory. Swam east and up the Ouse to sneak in a friendly with Equality FC at the Dripping Pan, £5 gate and kids in free, played out in the pouring autumn rain. Later in the season we suffered the New River Canal to play Arsenal (goalless draw, we were all sick as parrots from the parasites in the water), the weekend saved by a knock-up with Goal Diggers and Lush Lyfe FC raising funds with Playing for Kicks. Thousands in funds thanks to a tweet from *The Last Leg*.

TRUTH & DARE

The Grand Union Canal was a grander way to playing Birmingham at Solihull Moors; with lightly wrinkled fingers we leafed locally through Alys Fowler's *Hidden Nature* in the dressing room, charting her coracle course with our waterborne senses, charmed by her herons and blue-purple buddleja, her girlfriend and her oars. Plain water – calling it fresh is a stretch – is not our way but we will take it, not to our taste but we can breathe it, briefly. We are never without a crisp packet, the snap and crackle (how we miss the deep blue taste of Smiths Salt 'n' Shake). We map post-match chippies to keep our lithium in balance, our lithic electrolytes. Don't drink from our water bottles pitch-side – too saline for you, emetic.

St Blaise, patron saint of St Blazey and one of the Fourteen Holy Helpers, is known for healing illnesses of the throat. He stopped a child choking on a fishbone at his feet, even as he was being taken into custody by Agricola, the governor of Cappadocia and Lesser Armenia, on the orders of the emperor Licinus. Agricola had him beaten and skinned with iron combs, then beheaded.

We know how he feels.

Everywhere we go, they throw combs at us, a taunt at our vanity or our fragility or our femininity. In the hopes they will catch in our shoulder-length, waist-length, knee-length, ankle-length hair, trip us up, discombobulate us into bobbing the ripple of it. Is it OK? For so long, every away dressing room, they covered the mirrors superstitiously, as if that will disconnect us from the sea – as if it would make us disappear.

SO MAYER

They covered the toilet bowls with clingfilm. Slip in cameras and mirrors to find out how we pee. Please. We are magma, hot enough to melt plastic. To fuse glass. We have made ourselves who we are, not part-this and part-that, but all. All.

We shrug it off like our sealskins. Like water off a seal's back. Like we're impervious. Like you believe that. But keep making martyrs of us, and we will still keep winning.

&

We heard about CONIFA because of Barawa 2018, played in London as the base of the Somali diaspora. Only hints, whispers of the Confederation of Independent Football Associations. Cornwall joined that same year (the same year also of the first CONIFA women's match, Kibris Türk FF vs FA Sápmi, played in Northern Cyprus). From these islands, Ellan Vannin (original hosts of the CONIFA European Cup 2015, placing third when it was played in Székely Land, semi-finalists at the inaugural 2014 Sápmi CONIFA World Cup after a dramatic penalty shoot-out against Kurdistan) and the parishes of Jersey and Yorkshire were already members. We petitioned the Kernow Football Alliance to recognise us as the county team, Women's Super League runners-up 2027, to send us as Cornwall to the 2029 CONIFA World Cup, the first to feature a women's tournament.

'We say, "Tell us what your identity is, and let's help you represent that through football."' Paul Watson, CONIFA's head of member development.

TRUTH & DARE

CONIFA. For all our domestic success, it has become our obsession, a way out of Brexissues about European cup football, transfers, even county lines. This is not who we are: we are freedom of movement. We are a refuge from warming seas. We sing, as we have long sung, in the Atlantic tongues of Gaelic and Brythonic and Tamazight and Tashelhiyt, the ancient sweet sounds of Judeo-Berber from the Moroccan coast, in the Mediterranean sounds of Sard and lenga d'òc, Galego and Malti and Arabic. Your words, our words. On the pitch we shout in Sabir, the sailors' lingua franca of the millennial Med, heavy with Genoese, Venetian, Catalan, and Berber, excellent for swearing, undetected, one seaborne element of Polari, the definitive proof of the Sabir–Wharf hypothesis that sailors are the structural basis of all lingua franca. Our fans chant:

> Se ti sabir
> Ti respondir
> Se non sabir
> Tazir, tazir.

Let us translate: If you know / Then you say so / If you don't / Then shut it.

&

Meet Kelly Lindsey, CONIFA Director of Women's Football. We pasted pictures of her US career all around the St Blazey dressing rooms, adorning her portrait with shells and sea glass. We cheered on the Afghanistan women's football team she managed in exile, after FIFA stripped the country's football federation of oversight of the women's team they had sexually, physically, and legally abused. Captain Shabnam Mobarez and Mina Ahmadi were our outspoken heroes, even more after we heard that Mobarez, alongside players from twenty different countries, set a new world record for the lowest altitude match ever played, by the Dead Sea in Jordan. What salt she showed.

We once swam the bitter waves of the North Sea to Aalborg to see Mobarez play at home, making landfall, where else, at Klitmøller, before rounding the Jammerbugt over Skagen. Yes, and after that game, we did swim south through the waters of Kattegat, past Elsinore along the Orësund Strait, to see her, the one you always ask us about, at Langelinie pier, still on her rock despite being blown up once and decapitated thrice.

May St Blaise bless her and keep her. She had no comb to defend herself, only a rope of seaweed; maybe – maybe – her sealskin in disguise.

Yes, she is our sister. He stole her, the one who put her in a book, the one who put her in a ballet, the one who turned her into bronze with the profits from his father's beer. All of them, and only one of her (and yet thirteen licensed copies of the statue around the world). In 2029, the very same year as the first CONIFA Women's World Cup, the copyright expires and we will bring her – all of her – back where she belongs.

TRUTH & DARE

In the story, Andersen the sad sadist curses her – this cut-off part of himself, iron comb for his own back, his own internalised homophobia – to three hundred years as seafoam-become-spirit (albeit electrically earthbound, bound to do good deeds for the men who betrayed her). The statue has had seventy years.

It's coming home.

&

When we go to play in Sápmi next year – and we will – she will be with us, on the team, our talismanic number 9. There's no net she can't shred, no challenge in the air she can't win. But don't call her Ariel, that other lie naming her for the element she was dissolved into, residue of Andersen's self-pitying tears.

We swim in them, sea temperatures rising with all your human sadism, punishing yourselves to breathe carbon monoxide, to eat lead, to piss plastic. We take it all in through our gills, have learned to excrete it deep undersea, into vents already toxic with sulphur. Who knows what new species will rise to the surface as the Scillies finally drown. No more Road. It is always high tide. This time, when we swim north, it will be in temperate waters filled with basking sharks and swimming crabs and blackbelly rosefish and splendid alfonsino and tiny horse mackerel following their food *Calanus helgolandicus* come north from Heligoland. In Sápmi, in Staare, we will meet teams from other drowned islands and cities, from scorched places and refugee nations.

SO MAYER

At Mid Sweden University they will talk as well as play. We, of the sea, have to be there.

Kelmys on Ostrali.

If we can't play for Kernow, who now narrow-sightedly demand Cornish-born players only, we'll play for the sea, which knows no country. Our identity is insurgent as magma, granite-strong, stretching across the globe. Help us represent, CONIFA. Bring together our saline sorority; permit us our Permian sisterhood of the Variscan: Moroccan, Iberian, Sardinian, Celtic. We've been cast as statues and silenced, cast as villainous seducers and chastised. Shamed for our tails, told to jam them between our legs, which are called false because we made them for ourselves. Illusions, confusions; enhancements we haven't earned. Punishments we've brought on ourselves. Penalties, either way.

Sing when you're winning, they taunt us.

Ask the sunken lands of Lyonesse. The sea always wins.

vampire

I was a dark and stormy night.

Doesn't every teenager think that? Does every teenager have a mysterious Romanian great-grandmother whose family managed a cemetery in Bucharest before the war? Does that great-grandmother of yours, that ageless beauty whose hair is still pitch-dark in her eighties, have three passports and one set of enemy alien registration papers, all with different ages in which her date of birth gets a year later with each passing document? Does yours wear velvet dresses but like to strip a chicken carcass in the bath? Same, right.

Does every teenager wish they could disappear in the night mirror? I did, practiced erasing my face again and again, staring cross-eyed and vacant at the glass until I was not there. I was pale, nocturnal, bloody: a vampire. Running in the family, hey baby.

&

TRUTH & DARE

EXT.
Night.
Winter.

          1992   1932
    Bournemouth   Bucharest

I stand on the sea shore.

          I stand on the dancefloor.

Alone, nothing left.

          Nothing. Left alone.

Lightning flashes and

          The lights shimmer and

waves roll and

          music curls and

thunder slams and

          doors slam and

She is there.

          She is there.

Wet yet still

          Wet yet still

gorgeous

          glorious

uncannily familiar

          familiarly uncanny

like an old photograph

          like the new cinematograph

black and white against the sky.

loud with the song of the wind.

And I say

And she says

Who are you?

&

It was a dark and stormy dark and stormy dark and stormy night.

This is not happening.

You bet your life it is.

Living the cliché. Ashamed. Of living, however I'm doing it. So, what difference does it make? And it is dark, and it is stormy. It was a raindrop racing a raindrop down a family hatchback window, lit with the coastal city's Christmas illuminations and traffic lights, and now it's lightning striking the horizon. Zzzzzt zzzzzzt, like the board game Operation that I'm shit at, being short-sighted with no hand–eye coordination. How many organs before you lose. Because you killed him. Because you're dead.

It is a dark stormy night and it's such a fucking cliché because it's a dark and stormy night inside as well. Teach a kid 'pathetic fallacy' and you've made a Goth for life. In my long, dark coat and my long, dark boots and my long, dark hair and my long dark.

Out of my long dark boots now, toes holding the gritty, freezing sand like the edge of a diving board. The air smells

TRUTH & DARE

dredged. Dregged. Like this is the last sand they could find in the world, mined and trucked in. Metal and petrol and desperate, like a service station car park or a bridge over an A road at midnight where you sit and sit and do not jump.

Enough. Or, no, not enough. Not Goth enough, not bold enough, is it, to die half a mile from home, struck by the lone night bus that comes every hour outside a crappy suburban sweet shop where you used to buy ice lollies.

Ice in my veins. That's what they say. Call me cold, iron. I'll show them. Cold as the sea. Fuck. Slippery, this fake sand. They imported it, my dad droned on about it in the car. Because so much was lost in the '87 storm that blew a tree through my window and blew out our stove. He wouldn't relight it because it was Simchat Torah, and we walked five miles to my grandparents' house, me climbing over fallen trees in an ankle-length skirt and patent leather shoes that sliced my ankles to blood. Fuck. It's six years later and here. Sand sucking out from beneath my feet with the undertow. Even better than the real thing.

Hardly any stones on this pleasure beach, but enough for my pockets. Long, dark coat. Shoplifting coat. No pockets in the skirt I have to wear because I am told to. Erev Shabbat and a skirt is to hide your pocket, the one Lucy Locket lost. My boots on the beach. Will someone find them? Will someone recognise them? The stupid flowers I painted on the side in puffy fabric paint.

Pathetic, fallacy. Thunder in my teeth and skull. Keep walking. The tide is high so I'm moving on. Surf to my knees.

SO MAYER

To my thighs. Iron. Salt on my lips, in my hair (long, dark). Drag of it.

There's a line – call it a shoreline, an unsure line, ha ha hrrrrrrrrr – between want and need. A line between thinking *I did this* and thinking *It happened to me*. A line between being able to go back and having to go forward.

       washes up washes away washes away washes up
       washes away

line of the hips
line of the di   aphragm
line of the ribs
   of the ri hih   hih   hih   hibs
line of underwire

crossfire

light against dark
dark against light
striking
horizon

And then I'm swimming, twisting out of the coat, black shirt blackwet against my skin, firesmell; afterfiresmell, but why fireworks on Christmas Eve. Smokesore throat she is. Fire in her eyes reflecting the horizon. Arms around her like we were taught in the pool, only spitting salt as I haul, not chlorine, skirt tangling and tights ballooning. W-w-w-wet through. Her too, shivering in an evening dress, its silk a wave and sinking beneath them.

And then we are on wetdry land coughing into each other's throats shaking against each other's shoulders our bodies coming up out of our bodies with the force of it. Sea-it, sky-it, fire-it, death-it, fear-it, her-it.

Uh huh huh huh who are you?

Rain sluices salt from our skin, streaking the heavy satin of her midnight blue gown. Thunderwind fills our ears, steals my voice. Runstumble up the beach to offer her my boots. She refuses them as if they were garbage, unfolds from the sand my height and nearly half of me again, broad and raven-haired, speaking French. Her feet leaving long prints as she swooshes through the pushed-up sand, then up. On the cliff path, my tights fishnet then less, ankle scraps. My feet wintersoft stumble over gravel and I stop, boot up, before we rush the road.

Of course I had no plan to get back in. *Wash in with the rain*, I think, hysterical, bones chattering. By the gate she embraces me, some lightning heat in her skin. Singe and I want her to kiss me. Her mouth by my ear, shelter from the storm.

you saved me

no, you saved me

now, I save you

SO MAYER

Her lips quicksilver at my pulse. Mercury through my veins laid out like a diagram in biology, the whole tracery lit up with cold fire rolling and beading. Not alive. Not not alive. Heart beating so fast it has stopped being a heartbeat, thunder and lightning together overhead. And in the afterglow, she is gone.

Long legs along the road, her.

A puddle on the hotel bathroom floor, me.

Flooded brilliant with fear and delirious with thrill. Making it back through the back gate with its rusted catch. Up the service stairs behind the dining room where they are all still sat, sat still, sticky as pudding, waiting for their Sabbath bride. In the unlit mirror, all that's visible of me is the dinner table slap, bruise bluing where my cheek used to be. For my cheek. There is no rest, just. The wave and the wave and the wave in all my veins.

Undrowned, undead, if only so that I can see her again.

&

Of course that's not what happened. I don't know how I made it out of the sea that I never tell anyone I was in. Dark storms come in unquestioned, and no one's great-grandmother shows up as a vampire thrown from a refugee boat sixty years out of history to pour new unlife into their veins.

Even if you've just been to see Francis Ford Coppola's adaptation of *Dracula* and its soundtrack gives you aural hallucinations as you try not to fall asleep, afraid of what will come to you in the night.

TRUTH & DARE

&

	Orlando	Dracula
Early nineties film adaptation	Y	Y
Immortal	Y	Y
Does not age	Y	Y
Travels widely ...	Y	Y
... but attached to home soil	Y	Y
Ambiguous gender ...	Y	Y
... and sexuality	Y	Y
Relationship issues	Y	Y
Into bedsheets/drapes	Y	Y
Also into dogs/wolves	Y	Y
Aristocrat	Y	Y
Crusader	Y	Y

This is not my English homework. These books are not on the syllabus. These texts are frivolous. This is not literature, it's fripperies. This is not A-Level revision, it's silly. The chart isn't even in historical order. Have I even read the books or just seen the films? What if

What if

If

I fancy both Orlando and Dracula.

What is the vibration they both emit? *High strung*. Like Sherlock Holmes's violin. Like Sherlock Holmes. What is the feeling?

Did you know that Jeremy Brett, who played Sherlock

Holmes, played Dracula on stage?

Did you know?

'The Last Vampyre' (1993) is a strange late outpost of the 1980s ITV Sherlock Holmes adaptations, adding a hallucinatory scene that suggests the possibility of vampires, giving full range to Brett's uncanny acting, his summoning of otherwise states.

Folded and stapled paper through the post. A zine. Episode by episode, quotes and anecdotes. Poetry. Sketches. Did you know? A shoebox full of secrets. The photocopier ink comes off on your fingers.

The scent of toner. Burn bitter, rumoured to get you high. No more Tipp-Ex and typewriters, this is the big time, hot stuff.

What if

There is something here and I don't know how to find it. Think about what we're taught, the tools we're to use. Underlining, checking the dictionary, connecting the words. Don't say 'what the author means', stick to what the page actually says.

Maybe the author is a vampire, flapping at the window of the words.

What if Virginia Woolf (1882–1941) reads *Dracula* (1897)? I read it when I was fifteen. Half-read it, sort of read it. I wasn't ready then. Too many letters (epistolary, I looked it up). It was a huge sensation. Maybe Virginia's dad, eminent Victorian Leslie Stephen, disapproved of the theatrical Irish writer Bram Stoker and his scare stories designed to titillate virgins. But maybe Virginia and Vanessa, grieving the death of their mother

TRUTH & DARE

two years earlier, were drawn to vampire lore, smuggling the novel into the house. Virginia was Mina and Vanessa was Lucy, really, although they played it the other way.

The blowing curtains that herald the vampire's arrival make a deep impression on Virginia. Curtains are how she remembers her mother.

What does it mean to be wanted?

What does it mean to die, but not to die?

What does it mean to be in thrall, to be pinned down, to be penetrated against your will?

Did you know that Virginia Woolf was repeatedly abused by her two older half-brothers, one when she was a child, and one in her teens, after her father died? Did you know she wrote about it in her memoirs, but they don't teach us that in school?

You can learn a lot from zines.

What if

wonders Virginia

What if there's an immortal, ageless, beautiful aristocrat who *isn't* a mesmeric murderer and rapist?

Where's the drama then?

What if you take everything that's thrilling about Dracula and make it ... not a threat? And not threatened? What if there's no hunt, no prey, either way?

Sounds boring.

What if you give a protagonist hundreds of years and instead of enslaving peasants through terror and eating half of Europe they ... write a poem? About a tree?

SO MAYER

Orlando is Dracula backwards.

Dracula is based on Vlad Dracul and/or his son Draculea.

I read it in a book called *Vampyres*. I read it in an interview about Francis Ford Coppola's adaptation of *Dracula*. About why the film begins with Dracula on a battlefield, a shadow puppet figure killing other shadow puppets. Who are they? Ottoman Turks. Why? Because.

Orlando begins with Orlando – who is named for 'Orlando Furioso', a revenge fantasy poem about a Christian soldier fighting Muslims in Spain – slicing at a 'Moor's head' (the film leaves that part out) which an ancestor had brought back from a Crusade. Orlando will travel east, to Turkey. Dracula, having been a prisoner in Constantinople, travels west, to England.

This is a borderland. This is history. It is spring 1993 when Sally Potter's adaptation of *Orlando* comes out in the UK, and the siege of Sarajevo is one year old. Ottoman continuoso. Western powers still crusading.

&

The figure of the vampire is both aristocrat and undercommons, cultured prince and Eastern despot, Christian crusader and Jewish pretender, high masc and haute femme, the fixed definition of cisheteropatriarchy and a deeply queer and trans elusive presence, airy and earthy, lifeless and erotic. What do you do with a vampire?

Stake it. A vampire is a story about what's at stake. In my

house, it was an untold story, a story on the matrilineal line about the night, a story of generations of abuse that had to be intuited from bruised eyes and bloody marks and absent photographs. A story I inherited in the body I was trying to erase in the mirror, in the mirror of the sea. Like Orlando, I turned to writing poetry instead of committing murder.

&

English was my great-grandmother's third, or possibly fourth, language. From an upwardly mobile religious family who had moved to the capital of the new Kingdom of Romania, away from shtetl life, they made sure their fourteen children, raised secular, spoke French, the language of society and business. French, Romanian, Yiddish, English, in that order, I think. My great-grandmother, who read all of Proust in French, was reading Jackie Collins by the time I was old enough to understand that I should be asking her for stories. Her memories didn't extend to the fact she'd asked me the previous day what 'fuck' meant and had told me that I was prettier now I wasn't such a fat child, all in the same breath.

I couldn't, at fifteen, put together the fragments I'd gathered from her oft-repeated splinters of story, thrown into the air as she – a tapissière – tried to teach me (no hand–eye coordination, no patience) to sew, knit, crochet, always ending in bloody fingers and tears. Only as an adult do I realise why the American servicemen bought her silk stockings when she was an unemployed enemy alien in London during the war. I realise how she survived, alone, deserted by her first husband and raising a small child. I know that she would not understand me as I am now, queer and non-binary, any more than she understood when I was five and I told her, as she fitted me, tutting at my solidity, for a tutu I would never wear, that I wasn't going to have children, and wouldn't get married until I had – an unheard-of thing in our conservative Jewish community – an independent career.

Maybe I underestimate her, the survivor, underestimate our mutual capacity for (mis)understanding. The vampire who infused a sense of another world into my veins from my early childhood, with her strong accent, strong food, love of books and textile artistry. Not every detective story turns up evidence, especially in migrant families, fragmented families who lie to survive.

There are photographs of my great-grandmother, and of me, with our matching dark eyes and refusals to smile. Cliché, she would have instructed me, is the French for click, as in the click of an analogue camera taking a picture. A cliché is a fixed image, a film still in a frame that freezes what can be. A vampire is a white man in a dark cloak who preys on swooning virgins. Click. A vampire is a force of nature, stronger than death, crossing oceans of time to find love. Click. They say a cliché becomes a cliché because it's true. The dark and stormy night was real, on the beach I've never been back to without shivering, even if for years I would not admit to myself that the sunny, fun postcard scene – cliché – was where I'd tried to end my life. Something flew me off the beach and up the cliffs, shivering. Something as big as the sea I still taste on my bitten lips when I think of that night. A vampire is a story of transformation. Fire and water and earth and sky.

My great-grandmother was not a vampire when I knew her, just as, when she knew me, she knew me as a girl. Vice versa is, and was, also always true – she was a vampire and I was not a girl – because. Look, I'm telling this story.

to the light

We are here, strange to state. Amid fire and water, earth and air, all the elements invoked to stop us, here we are.

Barcelona, 1932. Muchaches en mustaches stepping out of the gaslit shadows, laughing. Dark chocolate in many languages, xocolata on the tongue. Red wine, the crisp of a cigarette paper, all the things our mouths are trying to learn, relearn. The difference between Spanish. On the tongue, whispered Catalan. Out loud, Castilian. We are learning, on these Barcelona streets that run, like Las Ramblas, paral.lel. Roll your own, roll each other's, and ask, Do you have a light?

¿Tiene fuego? Got fire? – not what we thought was right: ¿Darme a luz?

It means: give birth to me?

It means: give me to the light.

&

Do cinemas still exist in your future? If they do, have you visited? Could you feel it, that presence, the weight of light in darkness, of darkness enveloping light, that movement there

TRUTH & DARE

in the projector beam, dust or? That faint outline, sense of someone not there sat next to you, someone who saw this flick before or will: that flicker. That's one of us. Motes in the beam. Don't call us ghosts; we can hear you. We're as real as you are, or at least as real as those figures on the screen you swoon for.

Hold our hand in the dark if you like. Hold it to your lips. That faint scent of good dark chocolate, of Phantom Red (the favourite of screen and stage stars!) bitten from a lip, of Cherry Blossom worked into leather that has to last, of a twist of rosie carried from home, never to be brewed. Breathe us in.

&

Has it really been six years? In 1927, we went on strike and we were struck.

We struck like the matchmakers in 1888, the year that *Frankenstein, or The Modern Prometheus* is reprinted for a third time by G. Routledge and Sons to meet demand, seventy years after its anonymous publication. Slow burn for the story of a scientist who steals fire from the sky. Matches called Lucifers, bright and fallen angels of flame, made at a rate of ten million in a ten-hour shift. Throwaway fact.

Throwaway workers, the girls (so-called) who worked at Bryant & May were tossed away by bosses like a burnt-out Lucifer: fourteen-hour shifts, fined for any small thing, nowhere clean to eat and the fast–slow death of phossy jaw from the allotropes of white phosphorus in which the poplar sticks were dipped, like deadly candyfloss.

SO MAYER

They strike and they win, represented by the committee of Sarah Chapman, Mary Cummings, Mary Driscoll, Alice Francis, Eliza Martin, Mary Naulls, Kate Slater, and Jane Wakeling. There's power in the Union of Women Match Makers. They lay the ground for strikes to come, moving from the struck match to the South Wales coalfield. Yet, by our time, the Trades Union Congress discourages lady (so they say) members. Saying we lower wages so should have lower wages.

Yet, on the tenth day, when the General Strike was failing, we joined them on the line. The suits at the TUC were about to give in, until we stepped up. We: nurses, typists, waitresses, teachers, milliners, factory workers, launderers, seamstresses, piece workers, shop assistants, dancers of all kinds, servants, civil and otherwise. The unmarried ones, the ones who hadn't been pushed back into that old story, the ones who room with each other, the ones determined to be modern, to be free, and the maiden aunts, the spinsters in lavender, the old girls, the ones who drove ambulances during the war and kept the braces, the smokers, the spitters, the dappers and the flappers.

All the workers you don't see, the capped and coiffed, the softly spoken, the surly and invisible, counting our coppers because we couldn't get unemployment benefit, set anyway at a lower rate for us, and unavailable if we refused domestic service. We couldn't afford to live alone, and couldn't afford to give up our jobs for the queasy benefits of a lavender marriage.

So, we join the line for our lives, just like the miners who started it, and the transport workers who took it general. But

TRUTH & DARE

you'd never have read about us in the papers that you still twist, yes, to light your fires. Not allowed. We're not union, after all. We hold the line, but no lines are written on us. The suits chalk up the win, although they leave our demands off the board.

But in our boarding houses and canteens, at the tram stop and in the cinema queue, at the lending library and the nightclub, we keep talking about it. In the docklands, we hear tales told to, by, from cousins of the women who joined the Salt Satyagraha, guardians' permission or none. Click click click like knitting needles, like the telegraph, like a typewriter, like high heels on concrete, like a motorcycle engine turning over, like nail clippers, like the sprockets of the projector.

&

What are you watching on the screens of the future? In your time, can a marcelled head be laid upon a breast? May lips – touched or untouched by the new fad for Technicolor – touch? Is a glimpse of stocking, a sock garter seen against skin, still, for you, an indrawn breath?

Oh, we've seen stag films. We've appeared in them, sometimes together. There's more in heaven and earth, et cetera, and sometimes it was heaven. Nudies at the end of the pier, peep peep. They last about as long as a striptease. Which ... we can draw it out, but only the length of the latest tune. The peelers did for the peepers, didn't they, and now where's a glamour girl to go but the flicks, and there it's all above the collar and not at all hot. Except.

SO MAYER

What we are watching, in our cinema of forever. What we have watched so long that we have become its frames: a film that otherwise would have been lost forever, if we hadn't carried it in our bodies of light, modern Promethei bringing fire to you. A film that burned in the bonfires of Berlin in 1933 – but that is in the future, just, when we are first watching it in 1932, Leontine Sagan's debut film, made in that same Berlin in 1931: *Mädchen in Uniform*.

Muchachas de Uniforme, the Spanish call it. Look at the film poster, red and black, the colours of our anarchist internationale. Lipstick sticks out on the stars' lips, not so much a slash as a heartshape, as if the designer kissed the poster, kissed the two lovers, here and here. 'A sensational work, passionate and profoundly touching' reads the banner above the red frame around a red rectangle in which they embrace: Manuela, the schoolgirl in black and white stripes, her head upon the breast of the young teacher who believes in kindness, Fräulein von Bernburg.

It is the first time we see ourselves on screen as we see ourselves, at the centre of our story. Of course, not all of us went to boarding school. We weren't, most of us, born with a silver spoon. But somehow on the silver screen that falls away, and what we see is the kiss. Over and over. We read in a fan magazine that swooning audiences in Romania demand one hundred feet more of kissing. They wear the same black stockings that Manuela wears when she-he plays Don Carlos, when he-she pronounces – before the demon headmistress – undying love for the divine Fräulein, in the words used to herald hereditary monarchy, a salute for the rule of love: LONG LIVE FRÄULEIN VON BERNBURG. Live Fräulein or die fighting.

The words ripple around the cinema. Can you hear them? Our breath on your cheeks.

&

In Barcelona, we step out of the cinema and immediately rejoin the line for the next screening, rubbing one calf against the seam of the other stocking, one shined toe against the seam of a wide trouser leg. Hot for it. Here is where we meet, this deco decadent palace. The Coliseum, a monumental corner where Gran Via de les Corts Catalanes meets la Rambla de Catalunya.

What is being fought here? Gladiators in gym slips, demanding the right to exist. Refusing the military march that passes their windows, causing some of the girls to sigh over a soldier. Those of us who were soldiers also sigh.

On the picket line, it wasn't the first time many of our necks have known a placard, or many of our limbs have known a truncheon, or faced down a cannon. Some of us still have the scars from force-feeding. Some of us slip back into our khakis and puttees, our coveralls, cutting our hair back up well beyond the permitted bob. Breathe. A cosh in a pocket, a hip flask. Some of us throw a spanner in the works, put a wrench in it, lean our bodies on the levers of progress.

Some of us are witches.

SO MAYER

Yes, it's true. Which doesn't mean that the 1927 Witchcraft Act was or remains just or justified. Putting a book on trial? What nonsense. All we were doing was turning tail on the loving huntsman, refusing to go quietly, to be his prey.

&

Do you still speak of the trial of *The Well of Loneliness*? What about the trial of *Lolly Willowes, or, The Loving Huntsman*, two years previously? It's hard to imagine. Even by the time Radclyffe Hall faced the courts, the experience of our Communist witch sister Sylvia Townsend Warner had been eradicated by lack of attention. Written out of history. Her novel was the first-ever selection of the brand-new Book of the Month Club in April 1926, and it became a genuine bestseller. Became the page we passed from hand to hand saying, 'Strike, walk out. Rebel. Leave behind expectations, even if they are the devil's.'

It didn't start with us. Long – if long-forgotten – was the tradition of lending libraries in South Wales, with their well-thumbed copies of *The Communist Manifesto*. It was our chwiorydd of the coalfields who turned to, turned us on to, this new book as subversive instruction manual.

Of course, you can't read it, because it's banned. The original version, anyway. How Lolly and her cat finally win ... In Sweden, the censors cut the kiss between Manuela and von Bernburg from the film they called *Brytningstider*, literally 'breaking time' or colloquially 'a period of transition', as between regimes. Even when we think times are changing, that we are living in the flow of time, the times break us. The times refuse transition.

&

As we walk through our new city, down Las Ramblas, the balmy night bright, every iron lamppost reminds us of what happens to witches. Hung in effigy, at first, as if that was not enough. Back in the isles, as here, we lived close to the docks, the markets, the factories, the shipyards. Cobblestone walk home, lit by a gasper. Rumour had it that not iron but electricity, Dr Frankenstein's dark power, was what could stop a witch. Of course, a live electrical wire will also stop – or start – any human heart. Nothing magic about it.

The grand project of electrification reached and reached its tentacles out into the private night. Keeping ladies safe, they said, well-kept wives and daughters at least seen safe home by the guardian bulbs bowing their heads under their black iron cowls. More like coppers' helmets, the arc lamps watching us as we go about what we call business, and they call crime or sin.

Not content with enclosing cities and towns, wires crossed the fens and moors, turned into fences that cut ancient byways used by Travellers and lovers and others. Signs saying 'For Your Own Safety'. Retired brigadiers with broom handle rifles souvenired from the Karoo started meeting at their clubs, offering moustache-twirling advice to the government on next steps. Where there are fences, there are prisons.

SO MAYER

&

Witchcraft was a crime of association. Oh, if you could afford to live in squares you could love in circles, no one cared. Run naked and plural through the grounds of your country house as long as there was one of us to clean up after you and hide the evidence. But meeting halls and lending libraries, nightclubs and night schools, servants' balls and the Sally Ann, boarding houses and the omnibus queue. Picture palaces, dance halls, groves of trees in public parks. Anywhere there was more than one. Anywhere there was one walking alone.

Any cover was cut down, or used for the renewed Cat and Mouse legislation, those loving huntsmen once again appointed to detain us for our own good. Peelers peeling us out of our clothes, rozzers roasting us in windowless rooms and iron-sided vans. More of them, soon, than of us. There was mass unemployment and the bottlers paid better than the docks. Why not. Even some of us joined up, good cover. You can't be hunted if you're the huntsman. Better to strike than be struck.

&

At first, Agatha Christie, when she disappeared for eleven days, was accused of being one of us. Then she accused us of kidnapping her, trying to *turn* her. Bamboozling her. As if anyone has ever been bamboozled in, or into, a spa in

TRUTH & DARE

Harrogate. What a bath bun she turned out to be. Was she one of us? It took a beady eye and fine moustache to sort it out those days, when those we'd thought were friends turned informants and persecutors.

&

Gone to earth, gone to water, gone to air, gone to fire. The four ways of getting free.

&

How do you travel in your day? Are you still confined by papers and lines on the map, or are you as free as the iron machines moved by coal and oil and steam?

We – many of us – learned to drive motorcars for a reason. We learned to ride bicycles, and to fix them. We learned to crank a combustion engine, and deal with its crankiness. We learned to haul sail, to feed the dragon, anything that would get us out of there, wherever there was. Some few of us have even learned how fire can lift us into air. But for all our Promethean force, we could not leave. Not without documents. Not without *permission*.

Like we were screen schoolgirls in need of an exeat. And so, we itched in our starched servants' uniforms, for freedom.

You can't sail from England to Barcelona. It's on the wrong side, the Mediterranean side, a dangerous and long sail through the Pillars of Hercules. But the proscribed couldn't enter France or risk Portugal under Salazar. The shores of Galicia are forbidding: Finisterre, the end of the world. Cadiz, yes, but there was something haunting about entering at the site where Spain's Jews had been forced into exile in 1492. There were Jews caught up among us, as there were Communists and anarchists and inverts. Witchcraft was a matter of guilt by association.

&

We can be a borderless state. An un-nation. We hear that in Berlin, where many of us fled (and from whence many are now fleeing), Herr Doktor Hirschfeld has been issuing identity cards to stop arrests for (ridiculous to think it's a crime) cross-dressing. This person, it states, is wearing the clothing that fits their gender. The thrill and fear of carrying such a card. Of being identified as one of us. Of course, witchcraft is not something written in your census or employment records but upon your skin. In your privates, which they search and search. And the scars left by their investigations are proof enough to the next one who comes hunting.

&

Spain is but lately safe haven. Primo de Rivera. What a beautiful name for a terrible man: head of the river. The spring. It took a year from his death in 1930 to the spring that sprang into the Second Republic. A tumult in the streets that was then secured at the ballot box. Popular can mean 'by the people, for the people'.

Red and black nights above us, fuegos artificiales, the words we learn for fireworks. Petardos, bengalas, light writing in the streets. We do not see it, though, not in 1931. Except in dreams scribbled behind eyelids as we sleep standing up at our duties in the laundry, in the kitchen, in the sewing room, in the bedroom, in the scullery, in the garden, in the Big House.

Our strike may not have been reported by the Beaverbrooks and the Rothermeres, but the domestic labour shortage was their bread and butter. When they weren't inveighing against immigrants, it was against the workers not knowing their place. The tragic loss of all those servants to better-paid jobs during the Great War – jobs where you could go out of an evening with your girl, without the lady of the house eyeballing you – was solved after '27 by putting convicted witches to domestic work, safely barred in by iron and lit by electricity. One stone: two dead birds.

Electricity cannot stop us, though, just as we cannot stop it. We learn it, learn from it. We: mechanics, factory workers, Singer and Underwood operators, wireless listeners, switchboard operators, hair crimpers, chandelier polishers. Did they not think? Did they not see that, though we may not be Dr Frankenstein, we are Frankenstein's monsters, lit up from within by all the shocks that have passed through us, on the job and off?

The brilliant flare of chandelier light dazzling their eyes, maybe. They were so sure they were watching our every move in the flat brightness. But what we learned at the picture palace was how a beam of light travels, how it throws nerves upon the screen.

&

Tell us to set your fires and we will burn you. Twisting newspapers early each morning, we read that John Cockcroft and Ernest Walton used a proton beam to split the nucleus of a lithium atom. Thinking they speak only to the learnèd, the broadsheets report on their accelerator built of spare parts, wood, and nails, which answered to Ernest Rutherford's earlier call for 'a million volts in a soapbox'. We have one of those in the scullery, splintery planks that smell of blueing. No use to us anymore for standing on to give our suffragist speeches, so we fill it with our spare parts, our under-used capacitors: that we can do. Wiring things with spit and solder: that – like taking out the trash – is what we're used to. Lots we can half-inch, lots we can tinker with. We know how to flirt with our friends who work in the garage.

We experiment until we catch fire. Some of us do not make it, and we hear our smug employers congratulate themselves, over the dinner parties we wait on, on the success of electrical deterrence. Still, we light their fires, and one day in the newspaper, a twist: a blurry photograph of a positively charged electron, a mote of cosmic radiation. Carl Anderson captured this miracle passing through a lead plate in a cloud chamber, which is a short cylinder with glass endplates to contain its water vapour. Here was antimatter, moving across the universe. We could feel that, jumping across the spark gap.

A split atom, a positive electron: kinds of dissociation, unexistence, impossibility made possible. Like light itself.

It's not easy, allowing it. Disappearing into the filament, into the air.

So many times and ways we have been accused of being dissipated. So many times we have been, why not, a little of what you fancy and then a lot. Mother's ruin, a golden oldie. Lovely tincture of opium, twilight morphia, harder to get since we left the front lines, and then the passing of the Dangerous Drugs Act. Gone, too, pop! the sniff of the little brown bottle to deal with the monthly blues. Bennies, though, handed out by Cook like sweeties: to keep us on our feet while we're serving, speeding us up to a blur then dropping us into nothing.

So many ways to get outside ourselves. And passing – *passing* – as a positive electron via a proton beam feels like all of them. Vaporous, powdered, all surface. A heady brew, swirling gaseous cocktail through which you move like a broomstick, like a mote in the eye of the moon.

Smells like cracking the ice on the pail in the morning. Like the last match in the dish. Like forever-washed stockings that never dry. And then.

The Coliseum holds 1815 seats, and at every screening of *Muchachas*, they fill. The projector beam, the proton beam. We are stars of the silver screen, travelling as the flicks do: a little drop, a falling-through, and (having disappeared entirely) here we are. Greeted by the scent of dark chocolate warmed by welcoming hands, we sink into the red velveteen seats. Sucre, manteca, 'Hola y ¿Com et sents?' 'Encantat. Estàs aquí.'

&

We are all members of the welcoming committee, and we are all new arrivals seeking refuge. Here, in the Autonomous State of Catalunya, en llibertat, a freedom only made and maintained by reaching out, by opening the gates wide: to overruled Hungary, to dictated Portugal, to occupied Manchuria, to occupied Libya.

Ahem. It took us a while to hear it, that word: 'occupied'. Not just for lavatories, but what His Majesty does too. And His Majesty before him, and Her Majesty before him. And we also serve, even if we're waiting for the next screening or act to start, lounging outside or backstage at the Empire and the Alhambra and the Egyptian and the Alcazar, the Imperial and the Mogul, the Dominion and the Granada. The Regal, the Palace, the Coronet, the Coronation, the Princess.

And so, we listen across the wires to Sediqeh Dowlatabadi speaking at the Second Eastern Women's Congress in Tehran. Our international gazetteer and seer, she who spoke up against the Witchcraft Act, calling for our freedom at the International Alliance of Women's conference in Paris, the year of the strike. The year of the hangings. Has it really been six years?

TRUTH & DARE

With her, led by her, we oppose British interference in Iran; we support her boycott of British goods and imperial sugar. We see you, Vita, writing freely of your travels through Persia with Harold under the aegis of the Anglo-Persian Oil Company. While he joins Oswald Mosely's New Party, forerunner of the Blackshirts, and edits their newspaper, you somehow escape the gaze of the witchfinder.

The witchfinder is everywhere that Britain has its tentacles. Everywhere that rebels against them, as did our deirfiúracha in Éire, that other kindred Free State across the sea. Western wind when wilt thou blow, so we did, travelling light over Casement's old sea routes to deliver the fireworks. We follow Amelia with our etheric eyes as she flies into occupied Ireland.

We have to join together, by water, by air, by earth, by fire.

&

The old formulation found, in among the songs that Sylvia Townsend Warner was collecting for stuffed shirt Cecil Sharp before he, that Berkeley hunt, turned her in, is: as much land as you shall ride in a long summer's day. In northern climes, of course, a long summer day goes forever. The sun never sets, as is said of the British Empire.

Fire, earth, air, water.

We do not have that much time. We know we are here only for a long summer's day in the beaten copper of Mediterranean heat. Sometimes we day trip in our striped bathers and sandals to Sitges, where our invert hermanes have their Bohemian bars, where we meet the handsome playwright Federico who adopted our rational dress overalls for his theatre company. Oh, and gave us – or took from us – Yerma, our nightmare, the one they want us to have. His words won't be enough. Lorca will be taken from us, too. His earth, burned.

&

Yes, we are witches. We can see that future that is coming. We see it because it is already here, a long fuse burning. And still, we take up arms against it. Our arms, scarred from the big machines and the heavy irons and the hot engines and the cleavers. Arms seen below rolled-up shirt sleeves as we drive ambulances (again), wield cameras and weapons and canteens and surgical dressings and pens.

Listen. This is Sylvia's lover, our dapper Valentine, writing to her girl about coming over here and taking up arms:

> In your hand you hold iron, and iron is too old
> And steel, which breaks and shatters and is cold,
> And our hands are together as always, and know well
> what they hold.

War is coming, here, to Spain. But our hands are together, even around iron. Wherever there is power, we will break it even as it seeks to break us. We will fight for llibertat in all the ways we can, brigadiers with our own kinds of moustaches, with broom handles to beat back the fascists. For as long as we can. In the hope it's enough – not enough, perhaps, to save the nightingale of Granada, but surely, surely, his death will cause the outcry, the pushback. Surely all of existence will become resistance, when—

For we can see only within the measure: the long summer's day is truly only a train ride to the beach, a char-à-banc journey home again, sleepy with sun and sherry. It is cast about with darkness and limned through with bright fire, like in Carl Anderson's photograph. We can see only the traces that the future makes as it passes through us into the past, shockwaves that go both ways. It is antimatter, the future. Like us, in your future.

Do not call us ghosts, but call us. Softly. Offer us dark chocolate and your hand. Join hands with us in a line against those who would stop time itself if they thought that would stop us. Link – take – arms with us.

We are not naïve enough to believe that spark could bring us back, your flesh against our shadow dancing in the beam. But it is worth the attempt. Know well what you hold. Come closer. Got fire?

Give us to the light.

fairy

Like a fucking cliché, *Dead Poets Society* was the first film I saw alone at the cinema, fledged hatchling just about to start my first year of secondary school. It tore me apart. Sobbing so hard into my popcorn that I couldn't leave my seat till the other three people laughing through the matinee had gone.

I wouldn't say that cinema – or Shakespeare, or poetry, or the weird way they meet upon the heath – was what made me gay, but it/they, in their weird entanglings and gaps, made something of being gay. Desire and loss knotted together inarticulately, spoken only in quotation. Grief for having left something behind, having set something down, before I even had a chance to know what it was, but still: it was. A living green crown that was part of a costume eschewed before I'd even tried it on, but still. It was.

And I went looking for it, in all those places, the scintillant green fragments of possibility, weaving them together from a film here, a text there, an encounter, as a bird makes its nest, messily. Always looking for signs. The week that I'm finishing this story, I'm at work at the bookstore and two people walk in holding a woven crown of fresh twigs. It's a prop for a card game they're selling, called Pigeon. I take it in both hands.

&

Nearly a decade after I saw *Dead Poets Society* I read, with a startled start of recognition that tumbles me back through time to a film that my newly sophisticated student sensibilities say I should abjure, an essay where Richard Burt asks something like:

> Would Neil really kill himself because he's told he can't be an actor? Isn't 'actor' code for what Neil also is and wants to be, and is forbidden not only to be but to express, which is queer?

Sat there on the nubby sag of a student-room sofa with its wet tea-bag smell, sobbing into critical theory. It's not that words, or images, can make you gay, but they can take you somewhere that has meaning. That somewhere is almost-always non-linear, a tricky tangle of forgiving yourself for realising too late what you were stashing in your carrier bag not to look at in the moment but maybe later, because the image is too compelling, too painful, or both. The aestheticisation of the thin, white, hairless cis male torso of Robert Sean Leonard as he prepares to kill himself.

No one in *Dead Poets Society* is gay, explicitly. Burt's point is that what he names 'Shakesqueer', unlocking a million

'Ohhhhhhhs!', functions as a sign and symptom, a 'Don't say gay' euphemism waving at the Eurowestern traditional association of theatricality and queerness, rooted in AMAB actors playing female parts – and, in *A Midsummer Night's Dream*, the play that Burt points out was most popular for the nod-wink in American high school films in the eighties, they also play fairies.

'But room, fairy, here comes Oberon.' In *Dead Poets Society*, it's the line that notably moves from the stage – where such things can supposedly be contained as 'art', as 'performance' – to the everyday world of the school, as Neil mutters it to himself under his breath as he walks through the corridor where all is Oberon: surveillance and rule.

But room, fairy: this is the question at the heart of the film. Where is there room for fairies? Not in the choking white cis male privilege of the exclusive boarding school. Only over the hills and far away, beyond life itself.

&

That they kidnap children is a persistent anxious narrative about the Fae in Eurowestern culture. In *A Midsummer Night's Dream*, Titania and Oberon are fighting over an Indian child that they have kidnapped, a child who has no speaking role in the play and is barely characterised bar their racialised exoticisation: Oberon's jealous rage is why Puck espouses caution. 'But room, fairy' becomes the space in which the play's entire action unfolds: in the space of fearing what power might unleash.

TRUTH & DARE

At the heart of *Dead Poets Society* remains the imputation, barely refuted, that a teacher (Robin Williams) has corrupted an innocent, 'stolen' Neil not only from his family but also from the status quo. But teenagers don't kill themselves because teachers encourage them to read poetry. They kill themselves because of familial and societal homophobia and transphobia.

Compared to home and school, how can Faerie – Shakespeare, poetry, theatre, the heath where they meet – not seem the more seductive place to be.

&

Fairy as a term for gay probably starts in songs and jokes on waterfronts and sawdust stages, and other places where no one's writing things down. When I was growing up, the term I knew for gay was not fairy but feygele, a Yiddish word that means, literally, little bird. There's no evidence that it had this meaning before Yiddish made contact with American English, the little bird taking wing from the fairy, the fey in feygele a bilingual pun, maybe. We are in the realm of the whispered, the gossiped, the winked. But whatever constellation of affection, amusement, and effrontery may have scintillated in its in-joke, it quickly became a pejorative that could harm and even kill.

In a 1998 essay, Angela Bourke makes a tentative connection between a cultural understanding of changelings in nineteenth-century rural Ireland – fairy or goblin children left in place of human babies – and gay men, suggesting parallels between Oscar Wilde's trial and the murderous persecution of Bridget Cleary, whose husband believed she was a changeling.

See under: other. This is not that different from that other nineteenth-century catch-all persecutory term that pushes those it snares out of the order of the Eurowestern: degenerate. To be a fairy is to be of the old order, that which empire and the Industrial Revolution are genocidally wiping away.

&

Fae is the older order. It derives from fate: fāta, originally meaning that which has been spoken, the origin also of fable and fabulous, modes of telling inextricably intwined. So, all our tales are fairy tales, or are not tales at all. They are how we describe, and decide, our fates.

The spelling 'fairy', with an individualistic little 'i', is a mix-up with white supremacy, as Fae comes into English from the French fée, then blends with old Germanic words that give rise to 'fair', which encompasses light, bright, and white, then comes to mean, additionally and consequentially, both beautiful and just. This is classically English etymology, a cruelly utilitarian strategy, a whitewashing that turns what was a radical escape route into a reflection of the everyday imperial world.

The Anglophone fantasy of Fairy appears as a cultivated cultural realm in the late nineteenth century, a kind of putting the trees in a tree museum after internal colonialism has razed much of them through enclosures and the destruction of rural communities and folk knowledge. It's another realm to conquer. And this is exactly the moment at which 'fairy' first starts to appear in written texts as a pejorative reference to gay men, particularly those who are, or are perceived as, femme.

&

Almost certainly the first narrative fiction film ever made is *La Fée aux Choux* by Alice Guy, in 1896, in which the cabbage-patch fairy pops babies unstoppably out of cabbages for sixty seconds, refuting the tradition of theft with plenitude. That film was lost, but Guy remade it on 35mm in 1900, which is the version you can find digitised online, and then again in 1902.

There's something headily queer in this repetition compulsion, given the complex process of setting up, over and over, a trick film, combining unwieldy early film cameras and unwieldy human babies to produce a brief dazzle at once incredibly strange (why are there babies in cabbages?) and indelibly familiar in its iconography of the high-femme, winged, wish-granting fairy, who is both participating in heteronarratives of reproduction (what do all women wish for?) and moreover doing so in a polite, Victorian, no-sex-to-see-here way – and throwing fairy dust all over that in her extremely sexy corset.

Because if cabbages make babies, then we're free of biological essentialism forever. What could be more fairy?

SO MAYER

&

I didn't come across this idea first in Guy's film, which I didn't see until lockdown, but in Lynne Reid Banks's punky children's book *The Fairy Rebel*, about a fairy who disobeys her terrifying queen to pop a baby for her human friend, sans heteronormative conception. Banks's book maybe cued me to start collecting alternafairies, like the biting fairies in the early scenes of *Labyrinth* who exemplify the reversal of rules in its fantasy world: a one-line joke, clever but barely visible. Unmissable, though, on Christmas Eve 1993, was *Eastenders* legend Pam St Clement in a pink tutu and, of course, massive dangly earrings, singing the music hall song 'Nobody Loves a Fairy When She's Forty', although the internet shows that I am not alone in remembering this as 'Nobody Loves a Fairy When She Farts'.

It was startling hot pink goss to me that Pat Butcher was bi. Or rather, that Pam St Clement was. I wasn't yet tuned in to the in-jokes, the in-gossip, and seeing this familiar week-in week-out figure of the everyday as part of Channel 4's artsy-fartsy radical *Camp Christmas* was even more startling than Quentin Crisp with her magnificent alternative *A Christmas Carol*. The show's co-producer Frances Dickenson notes that it was this collision of popular and alternative culture that saw questions asked in the House of Commons, specifically about the inclusion, at his own insistence, of filmmaker Derek Jarman, visibly ill at that time with AIDS-related illnesses: a reminder that the 'safe' campness snowglobed by British variety on stage and screen has always had its green roots in radical spaces. Lily Savage was serving more than the drinks.

No one loves a fairy when she farts. Everyone loves a fairy when he sets down his crown and exits screen left, but not when he appears on screen and says, 'This is my body, living and dying and queer, and I will not go invisible.'

&

But room, fairy.

The Spanish word for film, película, means a little hide. It's too easy for me, sometimes, to use film as a place to hide from having a body. It's too easy for film – as a canon, an industry – to hide things from us: our history and its own. A film is a thin skin, a surface that sometimes thinks it's the world and forgets it's a magical cabbage leaf growing out of music hall and magic tricks. If it's not a fairy tale, it's not a tale at all.

There's no relation between tale and tail, but around fairies and asses it feels like there should be, a wiggling, waving reminder that what we make of ourselves begins in our bodies and has to stay rooted to them. Bottom comes from the same word as body. Arse was once pronounced ears, so when Shakespeare gives Bottom an ass's ears it's three silky jokes in one.

Less bosses, more butt room. Here's a funny thing about butt: it means end of. It's time to kick out Oberon.

Welcome to the Butt Room, irregular cabaret night outside time for one glistening moment only at the Rude Mechanicals Club. We're here to get pucked.

SO MAYER

No one can rule Faerie. Its only royalty is us, temporary: kings, queens, prinxes, monarchs. Butterflies who refuse to be pinned. We know power is a drag, and drag its own power. Nothing, not even film, not even fucking, can bring back those who have died under the hands that grind out the Fae, the fey, the feral, the fierce, the femme, the futch, the farting, the fighting, the fated – that fable made by the words spoken of us, against us, by those with power.

But where the bee sucks, the wild time grows: a moment only, yielding. Still a dream, but what a dream. And in the giving of hands: amen(d), amen(d).

Pornographene

We already had dicks for all occasions, more than you can imagine. Packers, strap-ons, stand-up-to-pee, dildos sans et avec sacks, first-flush baby-dyke kawaii toys shaped like dolphins and caterpillars and aliens. We loved them all equally, although we sighed over those whose 'skin tones' were not our skin tone or really anyone's, bought just because they were there and cheap and It Gets Better, but still they were off, never had enough range or realness, even the top spec. Didn't have that sensation.

So yeah, we've heard them say we started all this to get hard. But truly, it was always about feeling. We wanted tender, expansive skin, beneath which was the pulsing of blood and an exquisite map of neurons. Arising as connections and cascades engage. Engorging, sure. And gorgeous. We wanted it to flush at touch: to be responsive, even connective. We knew that much, that matter is only what it is entangled with. Think of silk, of *Bombyx mori*'s intimate knowledge of its transition, generously shared. Haven't some humans long felt that in their skin, whether we admit it or not?

We finally admitted that we wanted to find – not invent,

not create, not *fashion*, there's nothing new under the sun, darling, and haven't we learned that lesson – was a fabric that could circulate, a woven neural network pulsating with our reach for each other. A fabric that had circadian and other rhythms, that, in its own sense and senses, lived. Tissue of our tissue. Muscle, fibre. Semi-permeable membrane. All of it homeostatic, which does not mean still. Think of those moments when (it's said) time stands still, all hot breath and too many feelings and what is happening. With high levels of sensory stimulation and neurotransmission, time slows down. That is, how your brain processes time and space and dimension and movement changes. Like, really.

&

The thing they don't tell you about major scientific breakthroughs is boredom: the boredom that precedes and that follows, the repetitious tasks and null results. Afterwards, we could have been out on Canal Street at post-pandemic Pride. But there we were, in the lab, and not a Dr Frank-N-Furter to be seen.

We just wanted to invent dicks for ourselves and our friends and lovers and complete strangers who want and need them, and we're man enough to admit it. Project FabDyck *did* spiral out of control. What happens when you accidentally cut your cloth out of the actual fabric of spacetime itself?

&

SO MAYER

Truth or dare: did *The Rocky Horror Picture Show* make you want to be trans? It was certainly our first suburban adolescent exposure to transfabulousness, followed later by that *are-we stoned-are- we-lucid-dreaming* animated reverie of SpongeBob and Patrick, wearing reeds as 'taches, singing:

Now that we're men, we have facial hair
Now that we're men, I change my underwear
Now that we're men, we've got a manly flair.

Set that against the background hum of tabloids tutting teachers to death, reporting on 'cheating' athletes and death-certificate double-takes. And no shortage of finger-wagging science moral panics: cloning, GMO, mRNA vaccines, hormones in the beef and in the water. All those supposed less-than-nothings we were told to ignore, tomorrow's chip paper, yet somehow they add up to more-than-something: anti-(p)articles forming the weight of antimatter all around us, crushing us into non-existence. This was the era of the superhero movie with its dual and confusing love–hate take on the Übermensch and eugenics (same? difference?). Disability, queerness, transness, racialisation: difference only ever represented by ambiguous analogy, bait that gave like marshmallow when we bit into it. Is it any surprise that when we found each other at uni we called ourselves the X-Men? Because we weren't. Not superheroes, and not ex-men, but (the parapraxis hit us) men who had suppressed our sense of ourselves in order to get through. School, all of it. And when your 'friends' call you Frankendykes because of whatever you're up to in the lab, self-piercing and branding and tattooing, you need a better name.

This story would fit the It Gets Better mould if we could say we found a mentor, a tenured Frank-N-Furter looking to follow up on the Oregon and Stanford trans labs, funding our transitions in return for studying us, something we would have been fine with. Lab rats, regardless: running mazes, multiple-choice-ing, documenting our microdoses. We were lucky enough: PhD funding with too much teaching and late-night lab jobs to pay for T jabs. We researched DIY top surgery via *Nip/Tuck* and *Plastic Surgery Undressed*, spent hours casing the uni's teaching hospital by fake-dating medical students à la Sylvia Plath. Our locker was a shrine to possibility, featuring a print-out of Lee Miller's 'Untitled [Severed breast from radical surgery in a place setting 2]' and pin-ups lovingly trimmed from *Original Plumbing*.

So you find us, on one of those long, frustrated nights, sweaty like a petri dish and maybe that's why the idea was spawning. It started with chat about tit tape because there we were, using invisible tape to replicate the famous graphene experiment: making one-atom-thick layers of sketched pencil graphite for technicians above our pay grade to try and lever off the sticky static surface intact. The chat naturally progressed to the sweaty burden of wearing binders in the summer, and the need for them to change size when one is eating one's feelings of yearning and rage looking at twenty-four-year Gender Identity Clinic waiting times and going-nowhere government reviews and TwitTERF. And then we were off to the *what if* of post-surgical shrinkage for favourite shirts and tees, thus saving £££ and heartache, and oh what about T expansion in the shoulders and thighs? OK, maybe we were a liiiiiiiittle bit high, vaping THC out of the barely-opening vents on our breaks, because was it just our imagination or could we smell Pride welling up in fireworks and glittersweat and beerkisses and nitrites from the city streets and squares? And we weren't there, we were trapped in the National Graphene Institute, talking dirty in sterile scentless cleanrooms, feeling flat as our 2D research material.

Boredom being the daddy of hilarity, we were somehow off on a complicated pun chain, a veritable amino acid that helixed 'the gay gene' and 'graphene' and 'Manchester' as if the city had a genetic heritage and we were proteins on its gene switches. It collapsed into crying with laughter at memories of school hikes in the Lakes that inevitably became damp, rained-off, unromantic-yet-weirdly-erotic trips to Keswick's Derwent Pencil Museum. Somewhere around the twentieth repetition of the phrase 'giant fucking pencil ten feet long', it started to take shape: pornographene. Pun first, real-world applications second. They say that the sex industry drives the 10% of tech R&D that isn't driven by the military–industrial complex. So, we admitted it (first time for everything). To ourselves and then out loud. What we wanted was (deep breath): dicks.

The first time we'd half-admitted it was at the feminist sex tech hackathon that we persuaded our supervisor to fund us, nervous newbies, to attend. We weren't the only ones in that slightly awkward academic offspace who laughed when someone said that, like Russell T-era Daleks, what they wanted was to e-lev-ate.

Never too late. We spent a rabbit-hole weekend down subreddits and highlighting back issues of *OP* as we researched, very scientifically, phalloplasties. Harder to get even our scientific heads around than do-it-at-home double mastectomies; we'd memorised Fanny Burney's description in a letter to her sister Esther about her 1811 bite-the-stick, big-knife-and-a-prayer unanesthetised affair. Sure, care is better now in medical settings; anaesthesia, antiseptics and analgesics, fucking A. But the fact remains: is it really consent when under ether? And what of a punk DIY history, a drag attitude of steal-cut-and-stitch, of self-modding, suck it and see? Embrace the trace, the homemade, the heartmade, the Hard((l)y) Boys investigate. No point waiting for bottom surgeries, we'd have to win the lotteries.

What if. What if. What if.

Turn that energy from scratchcard wishing to doing something about it.

The 10% of science that isn't bored wondering is fucking. No one tells you that, either. Well, they call it 'experimenting'. So, we experimented. We had always experimented, this was just ... intenser. Possibly also for our neighbours. Rolled socks, plasticine, latex balloons filled with mod podge. A nostalgia trip with leather and horsehair. Vegetables, tools. Moulding with platinum cure silicon. Stolen access to a 3D lab printer.

Looking for that skinsation, that transmission, feedback loop of whose pleasure is whose going every which way. One week later, we carried out a black bin liner filled with a lot of takeout cartons, some UTI antibiotic packaging, and an unfeasible number of empty lube sachets, a freebie cascade down memory lane of club nights, sex shops, parties, Prides, and other people's bedroom tables. All of them called Sylk and Glyde and Lyck, even the non-vegan ones.

Thus our gap-in-the-market dick-to-be became Dyck. A joke at first, a codename for the project voice memos on our phones as we researched silicone–graphene melding, looked into superheated ceramic, reaching for something conductive, stable, load-bearing, elastic, and tear-resistant. Yes, we called the non-functional prototype Dyck Van Dyke, hoping for a jolly 'oliday and certain for sure that Dr Mark Sloan, being a suave gent and crime-fighter, would back our project. But it turned out it was a Diagnosis: Failure.

So, we stopped working on the object and concentrated on the material, thinking maybe a conductive, elastic sleeve would transform our ever-growing dickollection into the selfsation we were seeking. FabDyck was, scientifically, a great breakthrough – but a terrible attempt to pun on 'fabric', especially as too much of a good thing turned out, quelle surprise, to be a *little* toxic when used intimately. The concept, though, was sticky, like graphene tape. Graphene itself, its touch-sensitive properties already at use in our phone screens, was compelling. But it was the plasticity where the tape bonded to a few graphene atoms that caught at us, a superfluid sort-of (yes, that's a scientific term) colloid we kept investigating even when it was clear that it wouldn't automatically generate the dicks of our dreams. Its properties relied on a particle that we called a glue-on for its strong attractive force and its mechanism of exchange, what seemed like a deep loyalty to existing. Its anti-particle partner, which we called a muumuu-on, was described as the unstable one, quick-quick-slow to decay, but we saw it could be capacious, edging to infinity, with a flair for drama and, handily, able to penetrate deeply into matter.

So, it seemed that, down at the elementary particle level, in this supercool sort-of liquid, something even funkier than graphene was occurring. Andre and Konstantin, as we had never previously been allowed to call them, got what we were doing, and eventually we were upgraded to casually hadron-colliding dildos on the uni's coin. If this is the bit where you expect electricity to bolt down from the sky and bring the project to life, then *mad scientist laugh*. No Frankendick (as the press liked to refer to it, as if Sandy Stone hadn't called out that reference half a century ago) arose from the slab to electrify us. Instead, what we had on our hands was what we'd originally speculated about: a material that was almost-infinitely pliable, mouldable, and resizable while retaining integrity and plasticity, almost impossible to abrade, puncture, or burn. No more having to buy pregnancy pants! The collapse of bougie children's clothing manufacturers! FabRyk – the university's preferred, aka dickless, trademark – initially made plenty of people FabRich, but not us. This bit of the story is public, of course: how we released the patent into the ether to stop a corporation that wanted exclusive rights to manufacture not FabRyk but a proprietary 3D printer that would be the only way to generate it, and that only large companies could afford.

Reader, we leaked it. Ridiculous to think that our own IP wasn't ours to give. The uni considered suing us, but as FabRyk spread and stretched and swirled and swooshed across the world, as activist alliances – disabled, Black, trans, fat, pregnant, adolescent, migrant, working class, feminist, everyone who'd ever been controlled and excluded by sartorial codes – overthrew diet clinics and brand headquarters and fashion magazines and malls and museums in their new, always-renewing FabRyk outfits, while stowing what they needed in their almost-infinite capacity FabRyk bags and backpacks and pockets, as garment workers, agricultural workers, rag pickers, and retail workers rose up and created radical design and distribution collectives, as cows and sheep and mink and rabbits and lab mice were liberated and cared for, as parties and orgies and parades and games and hammocks and drywarm expandable shelters filled and slowly took up the streets, as sex workers DIYed skinsation self-sterilising condoms that caused no microabrasions (and could offer cervical and/or prostate health checks while they were at it), capitalism collapsed.

Just like that.

Capitalism collapsed and we partied. Our family. Kings and queens, queers and kin, all with their fingers in the raw stuff. The last surviving tabloids called it (again) Frankenfabric, and we said, yes: here be the nuts and bolts. Go wild. Thrift and thrive, recycle. Eat your underwear – while someone else is wearing it. Kick off your non-fungible trainers and let your feet connect to the fungal mats from which we learned the underlying structure of FabRyk. And so, they did. We saw huge festival tents that could expand to welcome everyone. Carpets that, compact to carry, could roll out endlessly, levelling steps and dips, offering just the right sticky traction-and-release for chairs and buggies and crutches. Clothes that breathed with you through a hot flush, that cushioned you when you were fitting, that hid or revealed as you needed.

Clothes that could, with some community modding, also transmit: sensory information, that is, which formed itself into feeling that could be shared. It was a post-amapiano DJ who made the connection, linking their outfit with their decks, pulsing the groove through their second skin, their gqom drop moving like live electricity through all the FabRyk in the club. People dancing close and consensual, so their FabRyk meshed, making polyrhythms as heart and footwork and bump and grind added their own backbeats. People crying with joy, people coming together on the dancefloor, people lost in their own movement, sweat running out the door and into the ground. The scent of it in the ether, pheromones stroking our olfactory epithelium as if the FabRyk had its own. Which it turned out it did, taking in or on esters, nitrites, terpines, amines, aromatics, and aldehydes. Collide:

what it got called, a colloid in constant connection and crasis, releasing and releasing.

It was something. Festivals, gigs, street musicians, kids in music groups, people running with music; soon everyone was trying it, the funk of it, union of sound and smoke and FabRyk, fibre and sweat and beat, the inhaled rhythm of the warp and weft. It's an old story. Some people say Stonehenge, like so many sites of closeness to communion with the eco-continuum, was built for sound, enhancing acoustics for those inside the circle through the stones' powerful reverberance and precise placement. Smoke rising. And, of course, people doubled down, holding ceremonies in ancient and new sonic architectures that contributed to shifts to a more survivable climate, in addition to the massive reduction FabRyk caused in raw materials usage, and, above all, a Bajau Laut collective's work on the incorporation of phaged polycarbon residues from the Pacific gyre into increasing the elastic capacity of FabRyk. FabRyk expanded, and the world expanded with it.

We could never have foreseen any of this, back when we were watching metoidioplasty videos in our summer-humid flat in Cheetham Hill, wondering what it would feel like. Already then, our five-sense thinking was expansive. Intuitively, we were led by our desire to experience fully and in collective freedom our own bodies and each other's, to imagine a material with this capacious potential. Yet despite all the cyberfeminism we nostalgically read in college, copyleft ebooks of Donna Haraway and Chela Sandoval and a treasured battered paperback of Caitlin Sullivan and Kate

TRUTH & DARE

Bornstein's cybertranserotica *Nearly Roadkill*, we had no idea that it could, like, really *work*. It's not so much that technology has a life of its own – although in this case that turned out literally to be true – but that ideas and beings tend to make connections, and then things flow and become and change. We never could have foreseen the buffalo returning, as the pipelines and their contents were phaged into FabRyk for basket-coiling and ribbon skirts. The rivers and the river dolphins and the ocean currents and sea otters and kelp and plankton.

When our parents were young, chaos theory was all the rage. Butterfly wings and their effects. Yet they still burned the planet to a cinder. As if their generation – or some of them, the ones who got power and money and clung to it – wanted to be agents of chaos. But when things started flowing back into being, they got scared. For every bit of five-sense footage circulated through the ether – and increasingly, through the mesh, although not everyone liked to be connected and they didn't need to be – there were the stark old-media miles of type we didn't see. Fossil-fuel-consuming emails and legal documents that snuck around without our notice, with no notifications. Maybe there were signs, but we didn't have time to see them. Literally. We were in a different spacetime, all of us who used FabRyk. Because the glue-ons and muumuu-ons were even funkier than our research suggested. They interacted, we knew that. Penetrated matter, bonded to it. Learned sensorially from it, from us: what was deep inside us, what bonded us. The buffalo that returned were *the* buffalo and their descendants as would have been and now are. Not ghosts or clones, but two spacetimes overlaying to become another. Ancestors came forth with their full lineage. Coal sank back into the ground. Time wasn't going backwards: times were existing together, a present that could have existed, had the past-past not been scarred by European colonisation and imperialism, was coming into being. Not chaos theory, but adrienne maree brown's emergent strategy. This always happened, long before FabRyk came to us, or we came to it. We all tore, over and over, repairable holes in the stickiness of spacetime, with our desire and our grief, with our visions and our touch, memory, and cum. All things that bring times together, braid them into each other.

We didn't invent anything. We helped FabRyk emerge out of the living universe. Without splitting a single atom, just letting particles get down and do what they want. Change, change, change.

They say we've ripped the fabric of spacetime in the same voice our teachers used when they said we'd ripped our tights. So what? We didn't stop dancing. We faced the same kind of judgement when we first plugged our earlobes with gauges. Listen: it's not a rip or a rupture – it's plasticity. Mutability. Wave, not particle. The skin of a belly, silvery with stretch marks. Scars healing visible.

They say we've gone too far, that people are coming apart, that it's us who have caused the divisions, the exclusions of those who have stranded themselves on the time-islands, increasingly unreachable shards not woven into the braided timelines. These time-islands, they say, are what have to be saved now, the extinction risk is to linear time, even to end times, to timelines in the sand, the straight and linear, the narrow path they are afraid to leave. Afraid of wolves they've made extinct, returning.

We say: wolves returning. Living in the colonial climate collapse timeline was causing fatal, unmanageable illnesses for so many, and so many others never said a word to stop it. We learned from that, from the suffering we saw and experienced in and from that silence. So, we were the first to admit that FabRyk has known, non-fatal, manageable issues. We shared our collider time with the silver-surfer team who first identified quanemia, a quantum effect that caused some older people's blood cells to struggle with being in the new timelines. Now there are 'iron-on' patches that top up your bioavailable iron, first made from FabRyk by a cancer survivors' group looking to address fatigue. There's so much that's adaptive about FabRyk, and so many beings who are adapting. They – you – could too.

We are not afraid of living with pain, illness, bodies that change from moment to moment, with fabrics and objects that need a little mending, a few adjustments. Before we were seen as scientists, we were experimental beings of safety pins and clear nail varnish. Holding the rips, stopping the frays, without being afraid. Without hiding them away. Never had we gone anywhere as queers without a little masking tape, a little spirit gum to stop things going *too* astray.

SO MAYER

So, with the living equivalent of tit tape and hair clips, we try to patch the braided timelines together, to keep them spiralling and entwining, growing thicker, as the hold-out time-islands try to take back control. From our perspective, we see spacetime, the living being of it, going extinct if they win. Temporal collapse disorder, complete and utter. We are tucked in our pocket pocket universe, enmeshed in the rhythm, trying to stay with the breath that takes its time, and gives it. Skin almost-infinite, shivering with implication and imbrication. We are our own collider, the we of us from that flat in Cheetham, the far larger we that our *what if* has connected us to, wider and wider until that first we, well, we're just one glue-on in a continuum, etheric and here-now with no line or flight between them, swimming in FabRyk together like it's the pool party from the end of *Rocky Horror* except everywhere and every surface is water and skin and self. Like playing French elastic. Over, *in*.

Oh yes, it's sexy. Ohhhhh yes, all our fluids are a gluey part of FabRyk now, sustaining it. We (it turns out) are coming spacetime. Energy is *not* finite. Why should it be when together we are not?

And if we have to go back and do it all again, one pencil shading at a time, one vape, one yearning, one check-in, one lube sachet, one orgasm, one research grant application at a time, then we would. We will. We are going to have done, and will have always been going to. Because, oh cosmos, if you could just feel how this feels. Because, cosmos, this is how you feel.

verde te quiero verde

First, our hair turned tendril.

Ivies, mosses. Perfect refraction at scale. Chaos practice, yes, everywhere. Grassy mounds, chin bryophytes, whorled herb around nipples, brushing knuckles, lining spines. This is not a metaphor. Maybe we had hybridised by inhalation, our apartments rife with plants (pot and potted) to ward off the pollution outside that was killing so many of us. By leaves we live.

As long as the soft, new green was under our clothes, seen only by lovers, it was fine. But our sappy heads caught the critical eye, brought out the bifurcating responses of knowing bros ('Science is built on questions, experiments, imperial – we mean empirical – knowledge, let us gather') and Doubting Thomi ('How dyou get it so green? Can I touch it?')

Implication either way: it ain't natural. It can't be. Explain, please. By what method? Medium? Petri? *You can't just go green without permission, without legislation, without a prescription. The oak tree is England! There are IP considerations!* Implication: we can't be abundant, self-fashioning. We can't – just – be. If we say that our bodies are our best laboratories. If we say we are our own evidence, that we show that our results are repeatable. If we say it is not a disease. If we say we don't need treatment. We are not degenerating backwards unless you see plants as lesser beings. It is not a trick or a trap or an escape. It is real, and it is evolution. Plants split from animals, they say, 1.547 billion years ago. Fungi departed nine million years later, a blip. A three-way split, the NIH says, relationships unresolved.

Is it too late? Never.

Maybe we could get back together. Maybe, we say, Daphne was always already the tree. Maybe the god – the god that's said to be of art and poetry and music, calls himself the wolf god, rapacious – tried to chop her. Chop her into her, into being only one thing, the thing he said she was. He took her laurels for himself. But laurel, survivor, persisting in isolated refugia during Pleistocene glaciations, keeps growing, long-lived and shade tolerant, high resilience to extinction. Even when cooked, whole bay leaves are abrasive enough to damage internal organs, so typically removed. Bay, bae, as in we cannot be kept at. We are a dream of the once-forest that covered every continent, the humid humescent sensate green lost under the grind of ice and fire, cut down by stone axes. But we know that we remain related, that we share ancestors.

For centuries those head-in-the-clouds white cis male philosophers bestrode the nature–culture divide as self-mounted colossi, earthbound, clod-eared angels with flaming pens all too ready to tell us which side of the gate we belong on, then turn their two-faced cheek to keep us out of the garden too. Theirs the root of the world tree, the tree of tales, etymology, deep deep, their pious and perfect relation with, as they put it, land. Hedge-high, maze and thicket, not a petal or an edible to be seen, toxic botanical sexism on top of everything else. Hello, hayfever is a product of (birch) plantation monoculture and (plane) sterile urban planning focused on cars. Clean cars, clean cars, move on. Everything thorny as the legal processes that get written by the winners. Treaties not worth the paper and parchment that were our kin.

You know that your heroes the Romans didn't have a word for green? Like, they just couldn't see it for the trees, which they stripped of leaves for their conquering ships. You know your Civil War was caused, in part, by same: deforestation for shipbuilding, ship taxes. You know that Iceland, the least forested landmass in Europe, had trees before the Vikings arrived and named a ridge they cut bare Þórsmörk, Thor's Forest, godwood gripped in volcanic soil, slowgrowing over centuries and cut down in decades for charcoal and fields. You know that the entwinement of agribusiness, deforestation, and slave labour has, let us use the phrase, deep roots. Palm, rubber, banana. Coffee, chocolate, mahogany. Linguistic monoculturation. The Greeks saw in solar shades, pale yellow to deep purple all one term, from the one precious plant that dyed them all: croceus, the saffron crocus. How close to Croesus, that golden miser. Your language, how Romantic, has been reaping us for millennia.

Stones do not want to be your quarry. Concrete yearns to return to sand and water. Glass drips and pools over centuries.

TRUTH & DARE

'They didn't know we were seeds': it's not some anonymous saying, but the first part of a couplet in a 1976 poem by gay Greek poet Dinos Christianopoulos. Do not attribute things to some vague ahistorical version of us as your rhetorical flourish, your authentication. Ancient secret. Dead wood.

You fear the trees. The grasses, the mushrooms, the whole unorderly sort of green growing lush and alive. Huddle in concrete forests in fear of triffids, pave over good earth to quiet your nightmares of walking trees, as if that could stop Birnham Wood from dethroning all murderers, all kings. Yet you fetishise 'the' grasslands, your shallow and convenient ahistorical 'roots', evobio fantasy abstractions, paleopsycho big-man Tarzan-chatting on YouTube about his spears and lion skins as if. Clubbable, right? Come lie on this looted mahogany and horsehair couch and tell me: why are you afraid of returning to the trees?

But but but, they stutter, we *plant* them, have you seen the evenness of an evergreen plantation? Have you sniffed the eucalypts as they colonise the wasteland? Clean-scented joy to all the girls and boys, delivered regular as Christmas while we're tinkering with photosynthesis, improving on the Green Revolution. More fertiliser! Rice up! We love our urban trees so much we keep them safe in cages.

Please tour our museum. Botany at bay. Roots? Shoots and leaves. We try to avoid the word 'native', the word 'invasive', but you know how it is. Things have dug in, spread like weeds – not that. Like. We are rewilding our language: did you know how many authentic dialect words for rain we have recorded (of course they are banned in schools)? We used to use cellulose and carbon, now it is the cloud. So ethereal! So airy! So ... canopy. Anyone can listen. Our mercy droppeth as the gentle dew from heaven and well, here *you* are.

Glowing, can we say? So healthy. Vibrant. Vivid. What style. Incredible resilience. Ancient secrets, right? Perfect. We should get recording. For you. For your, er, family tree, to pass it down. No, no, we don't need cuttings, we wouldn't, although of course it is extraordinary, it would benefit science. The planet. We could collaborate, we have the agreement right here, a DNA analysis? CRISPR are keen, yes, sounds like biting an apple doesn't it, ha, tree of knowledge, too close to home, right, yes, don't want to repeat *that* mistake or, I mean, it's a misunderstanding isn't it, why put food there and tell people not to eat? Knowledge should be free.

We're not for profit, we invest in community, our corporate partners are giving back, here's their no-slavery-in-the-supply-chain statement, here's their palm-oil-free certification. We don't call it greenwashing, we call it reparations. No, not in the financial sense. We're mending fences, not handing out the green. But we love your project. But we could be your voice. Grass us up. Share your knowledge. Just a little bite?

Said like the serpent – to the tree. Eve was just eavesdropping. Took it as read that only humans were animate, sensate, auriculate. She heard the hissing of summer lawns and thought it was for her, that it brought out the blonde roots of her melancholy trappedness. She had been thinking about hugging the tree, like in this self-help book she'd read: it said that the tree could rub off on her, bark better than bites, a curative. It said there was a scientific name for that. Acetylsalicylic acid, aspirin once derived from willow, *Salix*. So much ancient knowledge just awaiting its authorisation, its IUPAC name, its CAS number, its PubChem CID, UNII, KEGG, ChEBI, ChEMBL, PDB ligand identifiers. Eve checks the CompTox dashboard as she walks around the garden. Toxic, she sings.

She did not know the grass was screaming: not just from being cut, bled green even as it tried to sing in seed to waggle dance. In being cut for nothing, hay wasted under suburban sunshine, in being cut off, homogenised. Turf war, right? Grass misses the steppe, the plains. Endlessness and variegated, great herds of herbivores chewing and shitting, bringing seeds and secrets from other stops on their stampede, tamping them down with thousands of hooves. Windflowers, rivers, sweet smoke.

Sprinklers hiss and mist.

And in suburban aunties' gardens, it's hard not to dance in it, rainbow-bright. Ain't no mountain high enough. Petrichor passing through membranes so that we'll remember it in other places. The high forest of the dark sky zone. Here, leaves frame constellations and the Perseids fall like pollen into our open pores. Trees older than the Inclosure Acts, trees that survived the clearances. Trees that surely knew their northern kin in Birnham, messages passed from leaf to leaf, the memory of an uncanny crawl, a second line piped by eagles, watched by wolves and lynxes. And, stone by stone, the castle falls. The impassable briar, the uncursèd forest where those smart yellow eyes flit. Soft mosses sprawled into glacial erratics, our ferns unfurled unobserved and in communion. Nestle down. Allow softness. Lick of each other's leaves, root systems all caught up in mycelial messaging. We respond. Send heart emoji, green as pheromone. We release: nut, bud, spore, root.

Don't tell us we're too much all at once, that we're unseasonal. You made the damn weather, planet-straddlers. We just want to breathe. Do not call us guerrilla because we are gardens. These are berries not berets. We are not your cliché, click, the snip of your secateurs. Our arms are full of spinach and chard, okra falls from our fingers. We are here to feed. We are not here to endorse your green and pleasant brand. We are green, and present, but that does not – we are not turning light into chlorophyll in order to – cushion the stone of history. We know you pride yourself on your sadboy accelerationism, your privileged despair at how you made history and got left behind in it. Why be Moses when you could be mosses? The only future is a shared one. Let us break you down, turn your grey frowns upside down. Wash green back to its being. Increase available oxygen by consuming you. For a change.

corpus

There is no body.

This is not a philosophical statement, but a practical problem. One of the answers to Spinoza's question, 'What can a body do?', is: disappear.

&

If you need us, we will find you. Much like the A-Team, the Deadname Detective Agency (did we consider the T [in] Team? Yes) is both nowhere and everywhere. We don't do socials or have a website or email. We're annoying like that, invisible. Our main service is to offer the same to you. Need to erase the Google trail of your birth name? Bye-bye abusive exes, transphobic employers, political surveillance, debt. It can be as straightforward (ha!) as assistance with the hurdles of legal documentation, or an intricate plan to ensure your safety. We work on paper, at most. Conversation preferred.

There are unsurveilled ways of being in touch without using the public internet. Let's call it, for the moment, a quantum dead drop, nowhen and everywhen. There are portals, dataports, whatever you want to call them. We can't reveal our methods, you understand. It puts everything we stand for at risk. There will be a time when we can explain ourselves, but now is not that time. But believe us when we say: if you need us, we will find you.

&

It was something I discovered quite young: in the library with a candlestick, where all good bodies should be found.

My father was a weekend rare-book dealer, which sounds either wealthy or pretentious – white, either way. My parents were constantly whitewashed and class-shifted by those around them: perceived as less educated than they were, or as richer, accusations of money stuffed in mattresses. They registered as excessive and deficient at once, as if by leaving their birth countries, they had left or rejected the imposed British school and class system under which they had grown up, when they thought they were travelling within it.

Keep to your lane. My father's favourite implication of the Highway Code, definitional of Britishness. His speed of thought delighted and infuriated me, so much energy expended on what seemed like nothings. Long Sundays in the car to go to yet another antiquarian fair, estate sale, auction, random barn, car boot. Our boot packed with food, the particular scent of oils and spices making me crave the bland motorway snacks that would render me normal.

SO MAYER

Slim chance. I was, as I am, hirsute, tall, broad, and padded. Which is one thing, bearish, and was another in my summer uniform: gingham button-through that gaped and bound, leaving red sweaty lines carved into my skin. On Sundays, the deal was I could wear my England women's Euros 2022 football kit, and that I could have one crisp polymer tenner to buy the sports memorabilia of my choice. Fair bribe. My dad had form, an expert haggler because he believed money had no value. During the week he was an economics professor with a sideline in publishing neo-Marxist pamphlets in translation.

My mum was not in the car but not not in the car. We often listened to her philosophy-for-all podcast as we drove. You might remember *The Same River Twice*? I come by my Spinoza reference honestly, via her later-in-life PhD after years of teaching A-Level philosophy and English. Sundays were her recording day, the flat empty of my careening body and my dad's Abida Parveen on repeat.

So, we sped (crawled, in my view) along the motorway with the lunch she'd packed wigging me out in the back, and my dad repeating his wish list under his breath as I played *Minecraft* on survival mode on his phone. At the conference centre or national treasure or car park or auction house or house or occasionally even somewhere as banal as a bookstore, he would say, 'Synchronise watches', which I didn't realise for a long time was something people literally once had to do before phones that synced to the universal clock. I had my tenner in my polyester pocket, my hair back in a Grealish, and the promise of nuggets if I came back on time and didn't tell Ma.

TRUTH & DARE

Fair bribe, because what he meant was, 'Don't tell Ma I'm going to exceed my budget by ... hmmm ... double.' It was never intentional. He set out with a fixed amount of cash, which. Everyone had a Zettle, even the most old-school dealer. And what my dad was looking for was old school. He had a singular passion: books that were written in one language, but another script. For example, the Jewish scholar Maimonides' *The Guide for the Perplexed*, *Dalālat al-ḥā'irīn*, written using the Hebrew alphabet, but in the Arabic tongue of his homes in Córdoba, Fez and Cairo. Or like texts in Armeno-Turkish, which was used to get around the Sultan's ban on printing presses in the Sublime Porte: the pre-modern Turkish language, but written in the Armenian alphabet. A poignant remnant of a complex world. A whole history of trade, integration, assimilation, missionising, convenience, colonialism, mixed-up shit. He collected it. It started for him with *Hobson-Jobson*, he told me on one trafficky drive ('Dad, it's the FA Cup final, can't I stay home? Why?'), with Hindi words that migrated into English becoming an idiolect of their own. It wasn't called migration, though, but transliteration.

Oh. Anyway. That's not what I found in the library, or thought I was finding. I couldn't sleep. My parents were away on a Marxist study weekend in Manchester, and my mum's cousin's in-law's cousin's daughter was supposedly babysitting me, although I was not a baby but very much eight. She had fallen asleep in front of an Indian cop show on Netflix by eleven, like a lightweight, and I was restless. So, I took her phone, OK? No candlesticks available so torch mode had

SO MAYER

to do, to the library, which had a high-up tangled light pull that, tall as I was, I couldn't reach. By 'library', I mean a spare bedroom crammed with bookshelves. They acted – said my mum – as excellent audio baffles for her recording, which took place at the small desk set between and under shelves, and was crammed with hard drives, cables, noise-cancelling headphones, and Post-its covered in quotations from Hannah Arendt and Vandana Shiva. Sometimes I liked to sleep underneath it, like the dormouse in *Alice in Wonderland*, which was the book I was looking for.

Of course, my father had an elaborate shelving system. In fact, he had a catalogue. But he kindly kept the books he thought that I might like on a me-height shelf. Nothing there will surprise you: *Sultana's Dream*, *The Phantom Tollbooth*, *Sunny and the Mysteries of Osisi*, *A Wizard of Earthsea*, *Tyger*, *I Shall Wear Midnight*, *The Destiny of Minou Moonshine,* and *Alice*, which to him was in equal parts a guidebook to our local area and a textbook of both higher maths and anarchism. I liked the pictures of Alice changing size, and the rambunctious rituals, everything flying and careening. He had several editions, illustrated by John Tenniel, Tove Jansson, Yayoi Kusama, Anne Bachelier, Iassen Ghiuselev, Damir Mazinjanin (Bandersnatch edition), others I can't remember. As I went to reach for Jansson, I heard a – like the opposite of a thump, a thud being withdrawn. A whispered 'sorry', so quiet that it erased itself.

A few years later, I'd hear in a virtual exhibition the story of how Jansson created the cosy Moomins out of her childhood memories of the scary troll that her uncle told her lived in the stairs by her family's pantry, who would catch naughty children unawares when they snuck downstairs late at night for some bread and jam. It made me think of that moment in the library when I turned around and someone was there. Was not there, and not not there, a whisper disappearing into itself like a cursor moving backwards through text. Being a polite and curious child, raised by Alice, I said, Oh, hello there, and waved. Wavered. As the beam of the phone passed over them, they faded out completely.

A body in the library. The definition of a mystery.

I didn't tell my dad what I'd seen, for years. As you wouldn't. The child of an economist and philosopher, I was raised to prize rationality, storing the otherworldly in our shared familial love for Sufi devotionals and fantasy novels, which held equally prized status as a way of connecting to infinity.

It's logical, he told me, as I FaceTimed him from the uncomfortably too-short sofa in my student room, his face hovering holographically in the projection from my watch.

Just like the internet. It's networked, connected. You can be here, and then there's a short cut to here.

Oh sure, yeah.

It's just that instead of being with fibre optic, it's with books. You open a book and it transports you, right?

What?

I mean, metaphorically. Imaginatively.

Yeah, I get that.

Well, it's like that, but literal. It's a way of staying connected. Of keeping things safe. All the great bookstores and libraries hold keys that let you journey from one to another. Remember when you got so mad at me because I got lost in Livraria Bertrand, that time we took you to Lisbon because you wanted to spend the night at the Oceanário?

No, what I remember is getting freaked out by the rays swimming up to the sides of the tanks in the dark. End of my marine biologist career.

Haha. Your mother and I were quite happy to stop looking at all those shark documentaries, it must be said. We're so glad you're studying books.

As if I had a choice! I grew up in a bloody library.

Bloody?

What?

The body? The body was bloody?

No, just ... Sometimes the book thing is too much, OK? But tell me more about how your library is magic or whatever.

It's scientific, beti. There's a catalogue. It's just that ... it burned in Alexandria so now it's somewhat left to chance. We all contribute to the new ethereal catalogue as best we can, but it's haphazard. The burning warped things, so they are unstable.

Are unstable? That was like 2500 years ago. Wait, what am I saying? You're not serious. This is like some *Dr Who* shit. Are you just making fun of me because I liked the new N K Jemisin more than you did?

No, I'm serious. You really did see someone travelling in time and space. I wish I could travel back and tell you it's OK.

TRUTH & DARE

It was that line, which had no weight of the metaphorical, that convinced me more than anything. My dad the quantum traveller, who would use that ability – that ridiculous impossibility – to travel back to a nondescript Saturday evening just to tell me everything was OK. So, I agreed to check out the Sussex uni library rigorously, but found no key except the one to my gender and sexuality when I got cruised by a grad student, who buckled up a harness on me and showed me how to bind my chest. The week before finals. I was a late developer with a hockey-stick-shaped curve. To, ahem, my graph.

And so, the Deadname Detective Agency came into being, if you skip over the ten years in which we lost track of each other as, inspired, I switched from Eng Lit to linguistics with a side of sex diss, two codes that seemed to solve each other, and ploughed through academia to become a lecturer for hire, while Lough dropped out and, well, disappeared. Our one-week stand had definitely included a high moment during our post-finals blow-out in Brighton, where, sometime after our shoplifting trips to over-priced pit stop Perky Binders, I'd told them about book-based time travel, and they'd accepted it calmly, as people will after a bag of gummies. I assumed the calm was vagued-out tolerance for my weirdness, rather than the same wavelength, because I'd never met anyone on that frequency before. So, when they disappeared, I let them go, assuming that, sober, they'd looked back in what-the-fuck, and moved on.

SO MAYER

&

And so, you find us, via (on my part) a little transphobic line manager bullying and a little union activism, closely followed by a little departmental closure and a little sofa-surfing. Go ask Alice. I did, in the sense of Alice, the non-linear browser in beta-test, which led me both backwards and forwards, as it does, to long-lost Lough to help solve the case that would bring us together, the one with no body but an organisation called CORPUS: the Collective of Online Researchers Presenting Under-Recognised Sexualities&Genders.

No one loves an acronym more than graduate students, and it was one from my no-longer-extant department, now themselves an unhired lecturer for hire and a member of the collective, who messaged me to ask about the document, which also did not seem to exist. Linguistic analysis led to existential questions: not just provenance, but proof. Could this hinted-at-but-invisible page really be a lost – 'lost', given that here it was – poem by the legendary – as in barely known because he wasn't posh and none of his poems had survived into the present – war poet [redacted], he of the disappearing body, recently reclaimed by the Church of the Latter-Day TERFs as 'a brave woman soldier fighting for nation and empire, forced unfortunately into principal boy disguise'.

What the non-linear search engine that is my memory threw up was: standing with Lough under the blue plaque for music hall artist and so-called male impersonator (my preferred term: 'roaring girl') Vesta Tilley, who Lough was telling me had used her act quite ruthlessly to recruit young men to fight in the trenches, as we got drenched by a summer storm on what used to be the Esplanade in Hove. And that was, indeed, where I once again found them. Or find them.

&

Lough is leaning meditatively against the sea barrier, munching on a gluten-free vegan sandwich from Foccacia in the Rye. Grilled aubergine, red pepper, and hummus made with Norfolk chickpeas. Not quite locavore but not too many lost points on EatJust. I know what Lough's holding because I'm holding the same. Not an agreed signal nor a hipster affectation. Just the detective's stock in trade: coincidence. At this point, of course, neither of us is a detective, or would call ourselves such. As we walk past the abandoned adventure playground, Lough plays yes, no, maybe to my questions about their infamous app, DisApp, the aforementioned tool that could remove your deadname or other dangerous and unwanted previous from digital existence. About the app's sale for an unmentionable sum, and their subsequent (and, tbh, overdetermined) disappearance. The bare facts remain a matter of public record.

I won't write here what they told me, but it convinces me to delete even my incognitx mode browser history, and, by the time we reach the forbidden zone near the old water-sports centre, I'm ready to detach my device from the biofuel port on my wrist and throw it over the ten-foot plexigraph shield into the raging water. Past the last surveillance camera, there's an abandoned bench, its plaque weathered into illegibility.

Do you know why we're here? Lough asks.

Existentially?

Shit, I forgot, your mum hosted *The Same River Twice*.

They pull two ice cream bars out of a freezer bag.

Pharma-cone. Nice. From—

Under the counter, absolutely.

They tear off the insulating protective wrapper.

Technically the back room, I counter, following suit. Out front, Pharma-cone is Brighton's coolest, and also coldest, ice-cream parlour, although they prefer laboratory. They will make any foodstuff that you bring them into ice cream using liquid nitrogen vats and some patent technology. This being Brighton in the year of our Tory 2046 (not quite a thousand-year reich but no one would bet against it, which is weird given that every supermarket contains a fixed-odds betting terminal instead of a cash machine: you can literally bet your bottom dollar in the hope of covering your basket), we're still here, we're still queer, and the drugs still work. It's just impossible to obtain them via what remains of the health service.

But if you have a shit-tonne of patent technology and family wealth both, plus the surprisingly convincing front of a bougie ice-cream business, you can synthesise hormones and abortifacients, blend them with frozen snacks, and advertise discreetly in the very same places that the Deadname Detective Agency would, under my former student's Alice-savvy guidance, place its slogan (courtesy of Chanda Prescod-Weinstein's physics- and world-changing book, *The Disordered Cosmos*): 'Because we're the total weirdos who would care'.

Yes, Pharma-cone is elitist and expensive and less than ideal. It's a once-in-a-never treat for me, for all my showing off about the back room. Before I lost my precarious job, shortly after I also lost my parents in the COVID-44 epidemic, I'd been eking out savings towards top surgery (ten-year goal), but they were now covering the storage costs for all my parents' and my books and papers. As for the cash in the mattress, no such luck. I couldn't afford to take on the rent for the house in Oxford even when I'd had a job.

And so, when Lough asks me to move in with them, on our second date ten years after our first, I don't hesitate. I have nothing to lose. It's on this bench, then, that Deadname Detective Agency comes into being, without us realising it. That this story shifts definitively from first person singular to plural, although not in all the ways you're expecting or, to be honest, that I might have wanted. But by the time we stand up, T-tingling, I am in possession of two things I did not have previously: a place to live that will let me get my dad's books out of storage, and what's not yet a solution to my former student's question, but a clue. It has the feel of that crisp polymer tenner, unspent, a sweaty handful of potential.

&

Why were we there?

Because, although you cannot step in the same river twice

(my mum, being very into material philosophy, recorded that jingling intro you remember with her feet dangling out of a punt into the Isis, bless her), the sea is all one sea. Divide up the landward side all you like, even where it isn't cliff and cove – although the Seven Sisters are now down to three and some heaps of limestone rubble, Cuckmere more despair than haven – and water has no territory (yes, I know about drone-policed international shipping boundaries and pushbacks and island camps).

But it turns out we're not here to talk literal sea, so forgive my literalism. Lough is trying to address my lack of digital literacy. Thus the actual sea is Lough's explanation for the new non-linear internet (called web $\infty.0$) and how DisApp worked, then how they hacked it into non-functionality once the developers fucked with it. More importantly, it becomes their explanation for the bench, ex-esplanade.

We came here, remember?

They remember it for both of us. The dedicatee of this bench was the subject of their sex diss-ertation, a soldier stranded not only far from home by the Great War, but displaced further in memoriam – further still by the misnomer that offers a soupçon of deniability.

He was treated at the Pavilion, Watts.

What?

You knew that, right? The Pav was converted into a hospital for colonial troops. They, er, thought it would help the soldiers from the sub-continent—

Feel right at home amid the Orientalist fantasy.

TRUTH & DARE

Exactly. So, this soldier is one of hundreds treated at the Pavilion, which was a bit of a show pony, you know, 'Come and photograph how well we treat the noble savages. Look at the lilywhite hands that salve their brows!' It was only when the soldiers started stepping out with the young women who looked after them that everyone got scandalised.

That's what happened to this guy?

Not exactly.

Oh. Ah. He was—

One of us. Yes. It was a disgrace. He was court-martialled, sent back to the colonies. It was his English lover, a young doctor who survived the next war, and the fifties, who had this bench placed here in the seventies in the first wave of 'glad to be gay', near where he had retired. Where only a few might come to look, and fewer still know how to read.

So, you mean you always knew about [redacted]?

Always is a stretch but yes, I wrote my thesis on him.

How, when his papers hadn't been found then?

Remember what we talked about on this bench?

Remember? I have it recorded.

Srsly?

&

cs u n i r gna lv 4eva …

[Sung as a torch song, winning Pier of the Realm. Reprise for two drunken voices at the wonderseawall.]

Fuck me, that show was amazing. Defne Maybe is the

queeeeeeeeeeen!

We should—

Drag? As???

I've always wanted to be Sherlock Holmes. Call me Hercock Homo lol.

Which makes me – Watson? Nah wait, What's JohnOn …

C'mon, Watson's John is RIGHT THERE? Why What's JohnOn?

Because of the answer.

The?

Four letters.

Go on.

L-M-N-T, my dear homo.

Hoho. I love it. Subtle. I'm not subtle. Stumble yes, subtle no.

Hercock Homo? S'pose not. S'funny tho. Humble and stumble.

Ooooh, we need …

Sea!

Weed. But. Fuck. I'm bladder wracked.

I've got your back.

[Hiss hits the stones. Hits home. Bliss. Mixes into ocean as it seeps through the shingle. Deep. Deep.]

Watson, my pal. You know that stupid thing. On the internet, that 'my gender is crying teddy bears' or whatever? It's stupid but. That. There. That's what I want my gender to be. Listen—

Oh.

TRUTH & DARE

[Ebb runs through pebbles. Wears them. Where 'wear' means 'out', means to holes, means to nothing, to some beyond this. Attrition. Entropy. Things break down. Gutta cavat lapidem. Or something, something I once heard my Ma say, quoting someone else. 'Drip, drip, drip,' she said. 'The thing is: sand is time, millennia of rock formation ground into moments, eras and origins recorded in each crystalline grain.' That's what we're hearing, in the drag as it pulls us into each other, pissing and coming clumsily on the worn wooden bench, waves and waves of us adding to the endless spray.]

&

That's not the bit I mean, Watts. Although we were pretty cute and athletic back in the day.

Maybe we could—

?

Nothing. What was the bit you meant?

That thing your dad told you, about time travel via libraries.

What the f—? You believed me? Wait, no that's not the que— You DID IT?

Not yet, but I must be going to, we must be going to, because I wrote that diss that leads us to this bench, here, now. Come home with me, and bring your dad's library. We'll work it out eventually. L-M-N-T, my dear What's JohnOn.

&

SO MAYER

At my desk in a whitewashed room lit with sea dazzle is where I am now writing this, I guess, case history. The case of the missing body. Surrounded by my father's books, his, to be official, library. I can't tell you which book is the key, but it's here. It took me a while to work it out, so I don't give up that information easily.

It will have been the [redacted] affair that revealed it, I can say that. Sign-up papers: most likely his brother's. Family home: well, you know, don't you, because the Latter-Day TERFs had done their research. You have to give it to them: they're thorough. And they publish. Of course, they're also batshit. Well-funded, everywhere, and batshit dangerous.

So, what was our case exactly? Not just to prove that [redacted] understood himself as a man in the terms of his own time, and moreover was seen as one by others. We take that as read. But to find the missing poem.

How's it going? We're not yet able to say, but I know we will be. The Deadname Detective Agency will come into being, because it already has.

Sorry, this stuff messes with your head. Maybe one day we'll sit down together over a non-dairy melange at Café Corpus, a bookstore-cum-bar that will be going to have been opened by my former student in 1919 Berlin. Or rather, between here and there. Based on evidence that [redacted] had passed through the city on his journey home. Or maybe stayed. No one notices another veteran in Weimar Berlin, or another café. People pass through there all the time, they pass the time. Over a melange, we could talk, and it would make

TRUTH & DARE

sense, because we would be there.

We'd pause in our conversation as someone slouched into the café in high-waisted black cords and just-off-white linen shirt, crisp but not too crisp. Someone who could be staff, or a professor, or a film star incognitx. People nod like they know them. It's clever, Lough's look, their way of looking. It has come in very handy for undercover: not pretending to be someone else, but pretending to be anyone, invisible in their perfectly anonymous drag. Whether functionary or celebrity, low statusing is the key.

But I see them, as they browse the books. As they find the slip of paper inscribed with a poem, a letter, a pamphlet that they slouch over and return to you, [redacted], the dangerous message that ended your love affair, your medical treatment, your pay, that left its trace so that – this bit we can't explain to you – the Latter-Day TERFs could disinter and puppet you. You fold it with a shrug into the pocket of your greatcoat (I wear a matching one, rented from Angels), take up your walking stick, salute us, and walk away into history.

Case, closed. Nothing to see.

&

There is always a body, and there is always a library. That is what we are learning. Even when things disappear, they are – like us – still here.

ghost

I lived with a ghost for years. Not metaphorically. Something between a haunting and a poltergeist. I never saw it, but it did speak to me.

At 22:05, on Tuesday 18 June 1991, to be precise.

I know exactly when – a rare occurrence for me – because it was immediately after the final episode of *Twin Peaks* was aired on TV in the UK. My parents were out, and I was babysitting my three younger siblings. I was thirteen. Five frozen minutes had passed since Agent Cooper parroted 'How's Annie?' at the mirror when: the phone's ring.

It's the blaze across my nightgown.

My parents calling to check everything was OK. I went upstairs to look in on my siblings, and a high voice that sounded nothing like any of theirs said, 'Come with me,' as I reached the turn on the stairs.

&

I'd been aware of the presence for a while. In fact, my Nana (who introduced me to *Twin Peaks*, videoing it for me so I could watch it after my father initially vetoed it) had seen the ghost one day: it walked through a door that wasn't there (but had once been), straight through the wall, a couple of inches above the current floor level. She saw it from the corner of her eye as she was reading, thought it was one of us children, turned to speak to it, and it walked past her towards the opposite wall.

The washing machine broke down and the repairman found a silver chain bracelet belonging to my mother inside the motor, which was sealed off from the drum. He couldn't offer any explanation for how it had got there.

I lent a schoolfriend some tapes and she couldn't find them to return them. They were in my locker that afternoon, on top of a neatly folded sweatshirt I'd thought lost.

Two friends came for a sleepover and, while we were messing around trying 'table turning' with a stool (all of us holding hands), the CD in the stereo changed – not from one track to another, but from one disc to another.

By the time I was sixteen, I could place my hairbrush in mid-air in my bedroom, and an invisible force would hold it aloft.

&

Be sceptical, by all means. Doubt my sanity, my honesty, my powers of observation. Drive circles around me. This isn't about your belief, it's about my experience, about what manifested in me.

SO MAYER

&

I grew up with *Ghostbusters* and became a teenager the year *Ghost* was released. I read *Ghost World*. Being a girl, I learned, was about being haunted. A girl was a haunted being, or a haunting. Girlhood a psychic phenomenon, its existence dubious, its testimony worthless. Or, if we're going *Ghostbusters*, the world-destroying power of plasma streams where they cross.

In the words of *Ghostbusters*, though, I ain't afraid of no ghost. I am afraid of there being no ghosts, of nothing that exceeds Enlightenment rationalism.

&

When the film's hapless trio of paranormal investigators confront their first ghost, wreaking havoc in the stacks and card catalogues of the New York Public Library, Peter Venkman's approach is to break the silence of the library – loudly, wittily, and flirtatiously. Against the better judgement of his colleagues, Stantz and Spengler, Venkman attempts to woo the ghostly librarian – one could say, to bring her to life.

The disembodied, dessicated librarian, complete with hair in a bun, pince-nez, and silencing finger is a classic figure of all our anxieties about the dead-hand gatekeepers of the archive: we see that calm demeanour turn feral when challenged by Venkman, the rage of the institution when it's challenged to include other, louder, less conventional voices. Voices that are demotic, assertive, playful, alternative, and alive, and have no time for dead white rules about libraries (or poetic texts) being silently remanded to the page and the shelf.

What if, however, the librarian's only speech acts – her onomatopoeic vocalisations of a desire for silent contemplation and a rage when both personal space and an institutional social contract is busted – summon us to listen to silences, particularly to the absence of non-dominant voices in the archives. In another reading, this scene is an assault by three men on an older woman, a brash intrusion that denies the librarian her right to exist as a ghost, to read her chosen text in peace.

&

Shhhhhhhh and RAAAAAAAAARRRRRRRGH are potent enunciations that subvert dominant ideas of verbal language. Onomatopoeia and embodied vocalisations are associated, in Eurowestern culture, with the Other: infants, and people called 'primitive' or 'hysterics'. Verbal language is written into our culture as a marker of belonging. Sound is improper. Anne Carson talks in 'The Gender of Sound' about the association, going back to Aristotle, of femme speech with nonsense and gossip, but also with aggravating or even destructively high pitch and tone.

The RAAAAAAAAARRRRRRRGH screams into a void of silence. But there is also a concomitant shhhhhhhhh – a demand for a contemplative hush 'capable of being in uncertainties, Mysteries, doubts, without any irritable reaching after fact and reason', as John Keats famously defined negative capability.

&

Even the *OED* appears unusually haunted by the strangeness of the word ghost, the way it shifts time and eludes etymological straightness:

> Although the word is known only in the West Germanic languages (in all of which it is found with substantially identical meaning), it appears to be of pre-Germanic formation. The sense of the pre-Germanic *ghoizdo-z , if the ordinary view of its etymological relations be correct, should be 'fury, anger'; compare Sanskrit hḗḍas (neuter), anger, Avestan zōizda-, ugly; the root *gheis- , *ghois- appears with cognate sense in Old Norse geisa, to rage, Gothic usgaisjan, to terrify (see gast vi); outside Germanic the derivatives seem to point to a primary sense 'to wound, tear, pull to pieces'.

The root of a ghost is fury, anger. Its cognates mean to wound, tear, pull to pieces. In Old English, it seems to have meant to torture or destroy, rather than to frighten or scare.

&

TRUTH & DARE

The internet tells me it was 1994 when I first heard Kristin Hersh's song 'Your Ghost', three years after I heard mine. I saw the song as much as heard it, an MTV addict clinging to my fix while adrift on a family holiday. Something – something – about that video caught me by the throat from the first seconds. By the time Michael Stipe appeared, a punk angel in heavy eyeliner and mascara and a single hoop earring, singing harmony on the chorus, it was as if I had possessed, or been possessed by, the song forever.

The video, in which Hersh runs through a deserted house in a lucent white gown, washes the gown with a scrubbing board, and hangs it by a window to dry, reminded me of one of the Poems on the Underground, which begins:

The houses are haunted.
By white night-gowns.

The internet tells me it's Wallace Stevens' 'Disillusionment of Ten O' Clock'. Reading it now, rewatching the video, white night gowns mesh with Woolf's 'angel in the house', that haunting disembodied female non-being she tried to kill.

&

Katherine Dieckmann's video for 'Your Ghost' was one of two 1994 music videos for female artists, directed by female filmmakers – the other was Kate Garner's video, shot on Super 8, for Milla Jovovich's 'Gentleman Who Fell' – that made reference to Maya Deren's film of half a century before, *Meshes of the Afternoon*.

Why was Deren, who died in 1961, ghosting the mid-nineties? Lesbian filmmaker Barbara Hammer reports in her autobiography *HAMMER!* that *Meshes* was the only film by a woman that she was shown at film school in the seventies, and it seems horribly plausible that was still the case in the eighties. For female directors working with female singer-songwriters, there were few available precursors – certainly very few that would be faintly, possibly recognisable to MTV viewers.

&

If I walk down this hallway tonight, it's too quiet.

Perhaps we summon ghosts to keep us company. Call them like we call on history, to remind ourselves that even eradication can be survived.

&

I saw Hersh play a solo show a decade after 'Your Ghost', when I was living in Toronto. She sang of strange angels and gazebo trees, and then of femicide, Scots/Irish and Appalachian ballads in which dead women reproach the men who killed them, or for love of whom they killed themselves: songs known as ghost ballads, sometimes serving moral ends, dishing out spiritual punishment.

TRUTH & DARE

According to Sasha Handley in *Visions of an Unseen World*, some ghost ballads used real names and places to serve up their haunting. Turned into smoothness by centuries of singing (and centuries of femicide that keep them echoing), they still carry the charge of the individual, the local, the remembered.

&

Family psychologists have suggested that poltergeists are manifestations of the incredible misery and rage that teenagers – particularly girls of all genders – are capable of harbouring: a self that can literally smash the family home to pieces. The ghost as an escape velocity, a wild signal of survival.

Teenage girls don't just randomly manifest poltergeist energy because they're teenage girls. They're trying to say or do something we otherwise can't. Something *here*, something *now*. Making an invisible moment into one that will be remembered.

&

Another unbelievable story, one worn smooth by telling. Hallowe'en 1992, still in the penumbral shadow of *Twin Peaks*, I spend the evening babysitting for four children under seven: albino girl triplets and their brother. I had never met them before, and don't now recall whose children they were. Someone in town for a friend of friends' bar mitzvah, staying in a local hotel.

SO MAYER

When the parents came to collect me from home and take me to the hotel, I'd started watching *Ghostwatch*, a live investigation of the Enfield haunting (which took place around the time I was born). I carried on watching it at the hotel, trying to keep the children from leaving their bedroom to join me. In the lacuna between home and hotel, I'd missed the cues that let viewers in on the show's staged construction (30,000 viewers complained during the broadcast, so perhaps I wasn't as alone as I thought).

When I think about that night, I remember equally the shame I'd felt at school the following Monday on having to act as if I had known the programme was a hoax, and the persistent sensation that I was being (doubly) hoaxed and that everything that had been shown was real.

Amid all the rigged special effects (flying plates and so on), one very simple trick had convinced me most strongly: when the younger girl of the family in the haunted house spoke in the poltergeist's voice, a deep, resonant bass voice we associate with adult males.

According to Wikipedia,

> In May 2010, at a public screening of the film at The Invisible Dot in Camden, director Lesley Manning revealed that she provided the voice of Pipes the ghost after the professional voice artist hired for the production could not accurately replicate the style of voice she had intended.

TRUTH & DARE

&

I remember reading somewhere (but now can't trace it) that 'Your Ghost' originally had a cello playing in the chorus, but its resonance was indistinguishable from Michael Stipe's timbre.

&

When I think about 'Your Ghost', I think about it as a mourning song for family, friends, and lovers who died of AIDS-related illnesses. The presence of Stipe, the diffusion or derangement of heteronormative and cisnormative gender roles in the blending of his and Hersh's voices.

I put you in the closet.

Too often, queerness is written as a story of moving from a bad/bleak (forcibly straight) past to a utopian future, in which coming out solves everything (It Gets Better). It is presented as a story without a queer past, without queer continuities, in which queerness fits into normative ideas about time, from big arcs of history (We protest! We change laws! It Gets Better!) to individual lives (We come out! We get married! We have kids!).

What if ghosts are a story about queerness that fucks up time and ideas of history? What if everything they throw at us, every way they throw us, is about queerness manifesting through time, changing time?

&

SO MAYER

I remember narrating my future to myself, from when I was about seven or eight, sitting on the toilet describing myself moving through my student flat (thanks to *The Young Ones* for the concept). I can remember noticing what I needed to learn for that future, what moves I needed to finesse to get me there. And I remember the sensation that this was wrong. That I was wrong to want a future, let alone expect one – or perhaps wrong to be accessing the present ass-backwards, cringing from the smack.

Bruises ghost you, and then cannot be staked as proof.

I cannot imagine a past without trauma, and struggle with both the idea that I should want to, and that I shouldn't. It feels like self-erasure, and it feels like too much of a gift.

What if a ghost is the message that it can be both?

&

I don't believe that ghosts are dead people (and I don't think that all queer people are or should be dead). I think ghosts are the vital energy of histories that we ignore or suppress, within ourselves and within society. They are a protest and a resistance. They are a survival that asks us to look for what we're missing, what we refuse to (learn to) see.

Ghosts are the energy of another world pushing through – a world that's chaotic, anarchic, because it has never had a chance to take its place, or because (like Deren) it has been wilfully forgotten.

Riot ghost.

TRUTH & DARE

&

A ghost-writer is 'a hack writer who does work for which another person takes the credit', according to the *OED*. The moralising cuts both ways: the writer and the person taking credit are both judged and found wanting – ghosting each other.

Writing these jagged little shards of memory whose context and even content I sometimes have to look up online, I feel like what I need (what I am) is a ghost-writer of my own life. I need a self that wasn't able to form, one who holds memories coherently and can collate them fluently.

I would say I'm haunted by scraps and fragments of my childhood self, but that's inaccurate. Also (I would say and unsay) that I am trying to exorcise that self. Instead, I am holding the blaze and brush of memory, which is the formation of self, as it hovers in mid-air.

I held out the hairbrush, I think, because I couldn't hold it. I held it out towards a future that could look after it for me, as I did with traumatic memories, locking them away in my amygdala until I was safe enough to recall them. Believing I would get to that moment.

What if I – adult me, the me writing this now – was the poltergeist? A barely contained potential energy, a self that adolescent me almost couldn't believe was possible, so afraid that I would never manifest in adulthood that I was manifesting prematurely, as best I could, as a presence beside my younger self. Telling myself I would write this one day.

goes to see

for Ser & Sophia

unloosen the straps   the river becomes   footloose
& fancy free   as in   no imagination
– Sarah Crewe, 'anchoring', *garn*

Mersey goes to see.

Takes herself on an art date because it's been time.

She has been feeding the sea and not herself. She shakes out the shine of her locks, cricking her cracks – coal under the sandstone – against the sandbanks. Her sandalled feet show their lacquered toes across on the river beaches of New Brighton and Blundellsands, blown cool by the wind farm off Great Burbo Bank. Blown cool. She rests her wrist on Cinnamon Brow, giving imperial realness. On her right hand, the domed jewel of the Metropolitan Cathedral, on her left the stacked rings of railway tunnels and canals. Worked, work it. Time to.

Lamin Fofana's work of voices calls to her from among the blue-lit columns in Lewis's Building, sounding the Atlantic, its depths. *Darkwater*, he calls it, swirling with the songs sung to grieve and protest the massacre of ancestors thrown from the *Zong*. Thrown. Oh.

It's been time, and she has been still in her bed, shielding, heavy with sorrow. She remembers back to the last one before everything (and she) shut down.

Ferry across, Mersey. Ferries unite, fight for workers' rights. Every ferry connects to every other, so she steps easy – west to east, Irish Sea to North Sea – from her own Pop Art boat to the Broughty Ferry, gliding over the Firth of Tay, docking not far from, no joke, *HMS Unicorn* and Scott's *RSS Discovery* in Dundee. She's wearing the weather as a slicker, a voluminous raincoat so black it shines with rainbows in the wet, its billowing silhouette carrying her over the Firth as she inverts the peplum into a blow-out hood. And for her muffler, the haar.

In the blow, she comes to see the film *between a whisper and a cry* at Dundee Contemporary Arts. On screen, dancers dance the hornpipe in Clydeport, through the hallowed halls of the Maritime Museum, brought here to Dundee reel on reel to real.

Mersey pores over the blue book holding Christina Sharpe's essay on Alberta Whittle's first major solo show, *How Flexible Can We Make the Mouth*. On a postcard, she copies out Sharpe's words on Whittle's art to send to her friend:

> she dances, split, doubled, trebled, refusing spectacularisation ... is it she, the dancer, who haunts this place of

commerce – built after the official end of the slave trade but nonetheless in relation to it?

She does not send. She needs to think. She carries it back. She carries the book. She looks, she carries the look. She wraps herself in Whittle's grandmother's quilt. She stands, windblown, by the estuary, thinking about jute, Dundee's auld industry. The word 'braid', the word 'sack'. Sucks her teeth. Adds, pencil against the rain, words to the postcard. Ama Josephine Budge's wisdom from the blue book whose cover says 'MAKE / CAN WE':

Can I ever truly taste my own mouth? Can a dream be owned? Or a whisper or a cry or a memory? Or a crack cradling oceans in a cove?

You have to unfold the cover to read the title whole. Like the wake Sharpe reads in the ocean, which Whittle's films contain – no, overspill with. Five hundred years of overwhelm. Weather, capitalobscene, made by empire, the world and us crushed like sugar for. It breaks.

She cuts across the small island she knows to be a triangle. Curls up in her bed, feeling that coal seam. She is at see. Remembers. Goes back to the time before the time before, when more seemed possible, daytripping trans-Pennine to Wakefield.

The gallery is pressed concrete nestled in a loop of the Calder almost oxbowing, cubed peg in a curve. She is here

TRUTH & DARE

to see curves, to meander at the wave of her soak-off spring greens with the dripped-out raindrops soft shimmering upon their sharp tips.

She pours herself into Magdalene Odundo's exhibition *The Journey of Things*. Into that translucent *Drinking Vessel*, blown of very fine glass: a low, wide cup. Its swooping handles echo the swan necks of many of Odundo's much larger ceramic vessels, but it's barely a tenth the height of the nearby *Untitled*, the mighty half-metre of burnished and carbonised terracotta with a wide-open mouth, like a gramophone or a trumpet, summoning. It's the grand opening ceremony opening of the exhibition, calling out, hear here.

And there in the glass case near it, almost invisible, *Drinking Vessel*. The lesser-seen that catches Mersey's eye, always. A ceremonial cup of welcome, water to greet a dusty, thirsty stranger, the ancient tradition of the dipper. A glass-that-is-water-that-is-glass. Refreshed, she next pours her wet gaze into *Esinasulo (Water Carrier)*, hand-built by Odundo after her time apprenticing with Ladi Kwali, Asibi Aidoo, Lami Toto, and Kainde Ushafa. Incised, incisive. Mersey imagines carrying it on her hip, its toothed grins calling for water, water.

How this work calls her, to shift her neck, wind her waist, lead with her hips. The potter places the dance in her hands. Odundo tells Ben Okri in the catalogue interview that her works – *Untitled, Untitled, Untitled, Twins, Untitled* – are (Mersey copies this onto a postcard of *Untitled*):

just on tip toe and have momentarily stopped. They are staying still just for that moment. If you turn them or walk to the other side, they will continue dancing for you.

Challenge accepted. She moves her eyes with her whole chest. Looks over that sketchbook, fluted necks traced over and down a smooth-chested nude, looking like. The lip, the head, the curve, in and out. Odundo speaks it into being:

The human body is a vessel that contains ourselves, our being human ... There is no question that clay has made me who I am.

The potter's voice, heard in the video that loops downstairs in the foyer, seems to come strong from the mouths of her pots, to resonate in their burnished secret interiors. It overflows the glass boxes with their sharp edges, their 'Keep Out' signs. Even with all these pots to disappear into, the concrete presses down. Mersey admires the knife ring, cold metal like her flesh feels always on this northern island; what this island presses against her. She would shake hands with its maker, the Pokot artist who used steel and hide. Yes. Steal what you can('t) hide. Cut out.

She follows her glossy fingertips to water. The Calder and Hebble Navigation, cut to move coal in the 1760s, takes her as far as Sowerby Bridge southwest of Halifax. Feet flexed in stack-heeled vegan leather, she climbs the steep bank north of the town toward the moors. At the top of the incline, her lungs working like the mills once did, she stops and uncaps her favoured fineliner, 0.3mm notes for her friend, transposed from the book she is reading:

> Linguistically speaking, the resemblance is coincidental ... [but] the linguistic resonance between moors and Moors resonates with immigration histories ... [and] writing about moors frequently acquires an imperial flavour.

Savour that. She thanks Corinne Fowler, turning her page corner down. More later, she amends to the note that keeps growing, the envelope full of postcards and train tickets and Post-its and bookmarks. Poetry on bus tickets. It was Audre Lorde who described that. One day she will turn – she must turn – these fragments into a proper letter to her friend.

Wish you were here at Shibden, she will write. It's watered by the brook that falls down from Shibden Head, just off Ogden Water. Managed into the park's mere, it once gushed through a dry arch made for one Gentleman Jack, who called these Cunnery Wood. Derived from scullery, you say? A kitchen garden? Hmmm. That's not what I hear.

She sits for a while amid the winter deadfall, tracing the way this place has been made, not borne along, a crafted body wilding out of its planting. Is this her best hope of a date, a kiss? OK, Jack. Do you even see me, t4t? I'll spill ur tea. Now, let's talk coal. What fires the kiln (and the rest of it). So does dung, you know. The unburned ash residue must constantly be removed. Could you have lived differently, sir? Not without pussy, but without green. Entrepreneuring on the backs of. The tea goes cold. She is not welcome here.

She remembers instead where she was between the fires. *Somnyama Ngonyama*. Rubber tires, electrical cords, cable ties. Rubber gloves, can lids, polythene wrapping. These, their accessories, transformed in Zanele Muholi's hands and lens. Gelatin silver print on paper, a process also used to visualise DNA, but rarely, because silver staining involves radioactive materials. Everything is on fire, or almost, or has been.

Mersey surfaces from a deep dive that brings her to the Clyde, right into the Mac, into the Second City of the Empire. Here is self, portrait. Increasing the contrast in development. *MaID x, Durban,* bristling porcupine quills from Muholi's hair and skin. Surfing the web waterproofed in her scuba-ish fet-ish gear, tall and sleek, phone flashing silver against her surfaces, she hears the exhibition's curator Renée Mussai speak to the artist, and she transcribes in Notes:

> I've been thinking further about the idea of 'weaponising' one's practice lately, in relation to *Somnyama* – not necessarily in a militant fashion, but as a visually seductive call to arms, a protective mantle, a necessary reclamation. An occupation, manifesto, and invitation. These portraits are, essentially, about courage: the courage to emerge, the courage to reflect, the courage to exist, insist, resist, the courage to step in front of the camera – to literally 'face oneself'.

TRUTH & DARE

She saves. She'll send that email soon. Dear —— You showed me how to see, see?

Mersey comes to see, oneself, many selves, as the light begins to fade already at 3pm. She rubs her fingers above her fingerless gauntlets. Skin revelation amid these textures of what has been abused, what is called pollution. To increase contrast in developing: selenium, gold or sulphur tone the image, silver halides reduced to metallic silver. There, just that sliver. Fixed amid mined metals. *Sthembile, Cape Town*. She wants to break Muholi from the frame. She meets their gaze.

And sees herself, out. Thinks of Bristol, empire city.

She can't step from Broomielaw to Spike Island without hissing at the dry-docked *SS Great Britain*, for feeding bodies into the Australian Gold Rush.

Stops, balanced on one spike heel, wind glittering through her silver fishnets. She thinks of the other Spike Island, one wet westerly step away in Cork harbour, four times a gaol. Feeding bodies to Australia during the Great Hunger, it was the largest prison in the empire and the largest that the Great Britain and Ireland have ever housed. And now? A penal tourist attraction, naturally. One wet step.

She lowers out of arabesque at the Watershed, takes a Severn breath. Scent of coffee. Come the Revolution. But her destination is on Spike Island, named for it. A wandering complex of rooms full of people. She comes to walk around them: the show is called *Navigation Charts*. Lubaina Himid is *Naming the Money*, showing us how we got here. Here be map makers and painters, hear their voices. Mersey surrenders to the siren as she weaves among the freestanding, shaped board figures in their summoning colours, blue hats, patchwork cello. Hello.

Turbaned merchants wearing shades of indigo hold out hallowed textiles, cloths that are maps, this one a river system, that one with a hand and spoon. Remember hunger. Weave through the looms of the next room's installation, *Cotton.com*, here to there. Come closer to these small square paintings of conversation between Lancashire mill workers and cotton pickers on American plantations, the thread twisted between them as mill workers refused to touch the spoils of slave labour, even though they already faced starvation.

Solidarity. Mersey thinks about how the boards shaped into people-shapes have solidity because they are freestanding and standing together. Because shapes echo and repeat, and because each has its unique density of colour. She thinks about the deep indigo map of the river held by the figure in lilac and peach. She pulls her device – map, camera, notebook, archive – from the pocket of her frogged burgundy pleather jacket, folds back the bell-shaped cuffs, and finds Melissa Chemam's invitation to *Navigation Charts*:

> Walking through the installation seems to open a possibility for meetings across time.

Surely she'll send this one to her friend. Because the last time they saw each other was seeing Himid's work together, just a little of it, in *The Place is Here*. It's as if her friend is here, weaving just one step ahead through the standing figures, calling, 'Come on.' She can hear the clack of her platforms, the silk shift of her skirt. Wait.

A leap away in Nottingham, they had been *Dreaming Rivers* together, in front of Judah Attille's beloved film. What does the Trent dream? Lace washed white she wears tucked and stitched tight in a darted ballet wrap blouse over black bra, for its brilliant contrast, its historical revision.

Lacemaking had long gone from cottage industry to Nottingham's international export, Lee of Calverton's knitting frame working it even before the Civil War (English variety), until stopped by the strikes and burnings of cotton mills stilled by the Civil War (American variety), which also caused hunger in Nottingham's back-to-back housing. What is written in textile. These patterns are a map.

Here at *The Place is Here* is Himid's map *Thin Black Line(s)*, marking the 'moments and connections' between diaspora women artists showing in London in the eighties. Her friend, caressed by a deep plum knit, reads Himid's words to Rebecca Fulleylove, breaking them from behind the glass screen in her melodious, low, and carrying ungallery voice, so that everyone has to stop and listen:

> When I first started making art, I was like a lot of Black artists at the time – we were simply trying to make ourselves visible. We were visible in the street but we weren't on the television or the newspapers or media at all.

SO MAYER

Do you remember *Dreaming Rivers?*, she Imagines her friend asking her, asking if she heard, then:

a West Indian French Creole folk song ... delivered solemnly in that perfectly imperfect way only our mothers, grandmothers, and aunties can.

Her friend holds Rabz Lansiquot's words up to the light from the installation's screen, coved in a dark curtained alcove. Then puts down the screen and holds her hand. Together, they watch the viewers gather to watch Miss T, in memory no imagination, as she braids her hair, slow slow in her sanctuary amid lit candles that warm her skin in this cold island. Each strand, each crossing.

Mersey remembers feeling it in her own taut scalp, in the whorls of her fingers. Feels it now now as she lies alone in her dredged bed, remembering the hand that held hers, the one she always and never wrote to, the lost one, gone before.

Her own riverine eyes wet, and open.

curse

The season I turned twenty-one, I thought I was cursed.

Once upon a specific time, at an ordinary café on an ordinary spring day in a Western metropolis, a city that was not the one in which I lived, a spring day already warmer than even the recent past because of anthropogenic climate change, one person told another, 'You are cursed.'

It sounds like the cliché of a lovers' tiff, and I was in fact – or in feeling – embroiled in a bad relationship where curses were both cast and thrown, where streetlights exploded and dead moths were reanimated. But that is another story, one I was then trying – and still keep trying – to leave behind, leaving it there to come here, to this other city. Wherever you go, you take yourself with you: a truism, overused.

Which – overuse – is one of the ways that words become curses, in the vernacular sense. These are known in English as 'minced oaths', a profanity that has been blurred into supposedly harmless nonsense, like 'God, blind me' becoming blimey or 'God's hooks' – meaning the nails on the crucifix – becoming gadzooks. As if the words were crossing themselves against the curse of themselves. Minced itself – in English – being a curse of a kind, a pejorative slur, such that 'to mince one's words' means to speak indirectly or euphemistically and – but – 'to mince' means to exhibit camp or femme behaviour considered inappropriate to your gender assignment. So, curses can be words that have fallen foul of appropriate behaviour, and being cursed can be falling foul of those rules oneself.

And there I was with myself, the one that I had dragged with me, a self that these rules told me was a half-self because of heteronormativity, which is what the rules meant when they said 'love'. 'I now pronounce you man and wife': it's the classic example of performative language, of 'how to do things with words'. So long as they're backed up by church and state, such words alter your reality, as a curse does. To be under a curse makes it hard to trust words: not because they don't mean what they say, but because they do.

Words like 'beside myself', wanting the literalness of it: the ecstatic stepping outside of self I'd wanted from this getting away to visit my best friend in Vienna, so that there were two of me – or one and a half of me, which felt like more than two – awkwardly somehow fitting on a narrow, hard, curlicued iron café chair, a chair like the one Mona Hatoum uses in her sculpture *Jardin public*, with its triangle of thick russet hair placed in the centre. That is how we were, or were seen, sitting outside in the cool spring so that we could blow smoke up to the trees. We were drinking tea or beer or water, or all three. We were thirsty.

Four days previously, we'd decided to drive from Vienna to Prague, over 300 kilometres away, across a border strafed by searchlights from old Cold War military bases that lit roadside brothels. We'd driven through the night, met up with a raucous group of poets, partied with them through another wakeful night, walked around all day, then decided to drive through that third night to Duino, where we'd desperately wanted to sleep but could not afford to, so had driven through the afternoon and Slovenia and night back to Vienna. By the time we re-entered the city I was hallucinating with exhaustion so badly that I made my friend do an emergency stop so she wouldn't run over someone crossing the road – someone who, on second glance, was not there.

We slept, got up, and went to see an exhibition called *Traume und Trauma*, 'dreams and trauma'. So, it's easy to take this story with a pinch of salt, a measure that is in itself a charm or curse in so many fairy tales, but for sceptics a savour to help you swallow something, as we were salting our drinks with pretzels. It's overdetermined to be told you're cursed in Vienna after seeing an exhibition about psychoanalysis, after driving through Carinthia under chilling road signs that displayed a sunlit Aryan family superscribed 'Echt ist Schön', authentic is beautiful, put up by Jörg Haider's regionally and recently victorious Freedom Party of Austria. Perhaps it's overdetermined to be a Jew, two Jews, two queer non-practising agnostic Jews, in or returning to Vienna at the turn of the season decade century millennium, anyway.

And if I tell you that the person who told me that I was cursed, calmly told me across a wrought-iron glass-topped table, topped again with beer and pretzels, that he could *see* the curse around me, that he was a former Austrian soldier who had fought for the Wehrmacht, been taken prisoner, disavowed Nazism and militarism, and sworn to become a healer. If I tell you that he was at the café meeting a very young woman, a woman close to my age, who described herself as a dancer and a witch.

This is a difficult story to tell. Story is a difficult thing to tell: to tell apart from story, in the sense of a lie. It's like trying to tell apart the origin of curse in English. 'Unknown' intones the *OED*, but not for want of trying. Once it was thought to come from the Norwegian kors, meaning 'plague, trouble, worry' – but then from the Old Irish form cúrsaigim, meaning 'reprehend'. 'Don't tell stories' is a common refrain, a singsong reprehension from adults to children. Don't lie. So, a curse could be a kind of imprecation to tell the truth, or else. Trouble follows on the heels of a lie.

I was getting myself into something incomprehensible out of the blue of a spring afternoon, the blue falling between the green of the leaves opening on the lindens and horse chestnuts. Perhaps I should have been afraid (meaning 'to see trouble coming') and reprehended myself for stepping in its path. There are rules, after all, on whose fault it is when a strange man starts to tell you you're cursed.

But I was all out of afraid, I'm afraid. After months of reprehending myself for the trouble of the bad relationship, the physical threat of it, the ignored warnings from others, even before moths started reanimating in the dead of night, I'd run headlong into the immediate skinfear of getting stopped and searched at the Carinthian border when, on the third morning of our trip, we re-entered Austria from the Czech Republic very early in the morning. A tall, blond border guard joked about my friend's and my ethnically marked surnames as his colleague tore the floor mats out of the seat wells. It was a rental car, rented from a shady agency who accepted our student cards as ID when none of the other rental agencies would let us take a car from Austria to the Czech Republic, because cars with Austrian plates were being graffitied with the word FAŠISTA – fascist – since Haider had come to power. Fair enough.

We had paid dearly for that shady deal just after midnight the previous night, when the car had sustained a puncture somewhere in the Czech marshes. We had no map and no idea where we were, as we were following a detour to circumnavigate a flooded river. We also had – shady deal – no spare tyre. We pushed the car through the chilly, wet night into a town called Týn nad Vltavou, and waited nervously near a neon sign for one Bar Evil for the English-speaking breakdown service in Prague to send a local repairman. We had no Czech money left, and no mobile-phone battery. So yes, a day and a half later in the weak-tea Viennese sun, shivering that spring shiver as the cold damp of the earth reasserts itself towards magic hour, I had no fear left. Because having survived seemed so unlikely.

Being unsure as to whether I was alive or not, whether I was in a nightmare or not, was such a familiar feeling that I didn't even notice it.

TRUTH & DARE

That moment – being told I was cursed – was the beginning of noticing. A noticing by someone else that became, slowly, an inner noticing. I *was* cursed. The story that I spilled out, in response to being cold-read by an expert, seemed like a stupid story about a school feud, one that had also been witnessed by my Vienna friend, who remembered it better than I did. As our voices interwove, as past and present selves spoke together, it spilled into something more, a story of violent homophobia – which is, of course, a curse, a real curse. It was two stories, or one and a half, sitting in the same place: something bigger that I was just noticing, while still holding on to the possibility *that* this one scene, this one scream, was the curse, and I could be rid of it.

Travelling to Vienna had been an attempt to lift a curse. The curse of forgetting. And then what feels like the curse of remembering. You stand in a gallery watching a video installation, reading a text panel, and it feels like the gallery is inside your mind. It feels like pins and needles in your nervous system, in your limbic system, in your neural pathways. Because it is: lost connections being remade, optics inward. Remapped, so you can travel backwards to find what you do not yet know you have been looking for.

The next weekend, the poets, American and French and Czech, made a return visit from Prague to join a march against Haider, the sun already a little warmer, warm enough that the cops fell asleep in their vans. The cops against the march against racism. The cops' complacency that, here in Vienna, whited sepulchre where an old woman spat at my friend and me, calling us 'Äuslanderen', nothing would happen that would wake them up.

In Vienna, the city of Papa Freud and Onkel Kraus and Tante Wittgenstein, personal and social histories walk the same streets, but cannot be mapped onto each other. That slippage slips – and catches itself. Can we talk of the return of the repressed in the political sphere? Is there a social unconscious? Can things collectively rise to the surface?

Among the unknown-yet-known potential origins of curse, another Old Irish verb is suggested, with no explanation given: cúrsachaim, 'I seek'. It feels like magic, the exercise of deep language not only as cognate but as, itself, cognition. A curse could be that which seeks its own undoing; a curse could be that which, being laid upon you, sends you out to seek for redress, for relief. For your self, where that self is another way of being. A way that breaks the curse, that breaks the rules.

I thought I knew the rules. Which is perhaps why I was even less prepared to be given instructions on lifting the curse than to be told I was cursed. Less prepared still for what they were. Cynical little me, teen tarot reader to supplement babysitting money, I knew a cold read in my bones. But there was no request for cash, nor assignations. Nothing owed to this upright, grey-haired man who walked with a stick, whom I never met again, who never told me his name, only his former rank, his own curse to bear. He told me I had to move my body to shake off the bad energy, spend time in community spaces that were meaningful to me, and give my energy to them. If I wanted to do something concrete and immediate, he said, I could donate just a bit more money than I could afford to one of these places, but it had to be completely secret, a mission I would subsequently undertake with ridiculous covert panache.

Does it sound too easy? At the time it seemed like magic, the folk tale moment of being handed what you didn't know you needed. And it was magic: the only magic I believe in. And by magic, I mean accountability, or facing up to yourself and doing the hard shit. I don't have an answer to the question of why, on that day in that place, that man – with his terrible history – decided to talk to me, to share with me the secret of facing up to a differently terrible history. Maybe just by looking, with his terrible experience of such looking, he had identified my friend and me as Jewish, as the border guard had done before he even took our passports. Maybe, unlike the guard, he was seeking something from us too, some undoing of a curse. Or maybe that assumption is too easy. He and his friend paid for our drinks and left before we could ask them more.

The next day, being young and tired and vivid with holiday, my friend and I decided to find the best – as opposed to the most echt, authentic – Sachertorte in Vienna by eating eight slices of the ridiculously rich imperial dessert. Seeking has to start somewhere. Sprung with sugar, we then left the august Innere Stadt, the iced wedding cake heart of the old city, and walked northeast, past the Sigmund Freud Museum, heading almost to the Ringstraße, the ring road that demarcates the inner and outer city, where we reached the imposing industrial redbrick of the Werkstätten- und Kulturhaus, or Workshops and Cultural Centre, known as WUK.

Our guide told us the history of the 12,000 square metre former Hapsburg locomotive factory, which had been squatted by artists. There, they put on events, ran community education programmes, and slowly restored the vast complex, eventually, cunningly, as in a fairy tale, persuading the city to legalise their custodianship of the building. By the austere entrance, which still bore the incised stonework naming the factory's training 'school', where working-class children had been apprenticed to the factory, there was now a free nursery, next to a day centre for older people with dementia, next to a language class for recently arrived refugees.

Curse most likely derives from the Latin cursus, meaning 'order' and used in church Latin to refer to the order of prayers. The Old Irish cúrsagaid probably itself derives from a Latin term, curas agere, which can be glossed as 'to exercise control'. Cursus and curas, order and control, church and state. Who write the dictionaries, after all. Maybe a curse is a word that can't escape its origin, that ties itself in tighter knots of containment the more it tries to wriggle free, whether through magical thinking or imagined transgression. Maybe to be cursed is to start to realise you are trapped in the tales you have been told. It wasn't a fairy tale, but I did receive a gift: the gift of a lifetime's work to give my self, to move my self, both of these towards a future rooted in *not* running from my past. Squatting in the vacancies of my self, slowly restoring my self, opening myself up.

TRUTH & DARE

The season I turned twenty-one, I went to Vienna and left with the knowledge I was cursed, without which I'd never have known that curses could be ended. It wasn't magic, but I do believe – as I did in that moment – that energetic resonance between people, happening in specific time and place, is real, a real that is not echt, that is messy and partial and doesn't care about being authenticated by power, a strange and slippery real that is the realm of the curse, and of its ending. Art can take you there, or dance, or sleeplessness, or friendship, or smoke spiralling against the disappearing blue of the sky.

I don't believe it's magic, that movement, but that it's work. Rehearsal, practice. Listening like that comes from concerted labour – even between strangers – to attune using micro-movements, breath and sense information, so that the risk can be taken, something honest and profound can be shared. What you do with a curse is ending.

Hot Mess Observation

Mass Observation has a history when it comes to everyday disasters. It was founded in 1937, after all. In March 2020, Mass Observation began to issue special COVID Directive questionnaires to its regular contributors, as well as calling more widely for anyone in the then-UK to continue to submit their 12 May diaries from lockdowns.

Through all the subsequent epidemics, political disorders, natural disasters, and apocalyptic events of the post-Capitalocene, starting from the dissolution of the union recorded by the Venerable Gwyneth in the Bold as Love *chronicles, the surviving staff of Mass Observation continued to call for and collect submissions, which arrived to their offices in Sussex despite the eventual collapse of the national postal service, rail and road travel, and, after peak oil, internet access.*

Since the Green Re-evolution, community researchers have been literally raking through the archives of Mass Observation to understand the experience of life in the isles before the cross-channel renewables grid and food exchanges were collaboratively constructed by people arriving in small boats. Many reports have been generated and shared from the

TRUTH & DARE

records left for us by those who experienced the Dark Times, the so-called second dark ages, offering reminders to us to keep the balance lest we fall back into excess and exclusion.

One story, however, has been quietly kept back for fear it will cast aspersions on us as researchers, and/or on those whose words form our research. But this is thinking from before the Dark Times: a fear of the queer boundless dimension of the cosmos of which we are part. Fear deprives us of the fullness of our shared experience, and so we speak out.

Here, for the first time, we transmit those rare Mass Observation entries that give us glimpses of the emergent, non-linear Dark Times phenomenon (or phenomena) we have named the Burd Gurls, as per the entry titled 'Shanty'. Due to the collapse of shelving as well as services, we have not been able to determine dates of submission, and so are presenting these in the reverse order in which – working down through the shifting stacks – they were found.

These entries represent a vanishingly small percentage of the total, but, based on the locations and incidents to which they refer, they appear to document a phenomenon dispersed across the entirety of the isles and the time period. The writers share nothing in common – or so we thought, before we recalled that both in and before the Dark Times, open-field gender and sexuality were considered non-normative, and often cruelly and incomprehensibly policed as such. Brought up short by this reminder of the limitations of our historical perspective, we offer no interpretation, just share the unadorned, unedited words of our chosen ancestors.

SO MAYER

One note: although it took us many meetings and discussions to admit it, each of us, on reading these entries, hears or feels a shared music running beneath them. Impossible not to move to, to be moved by. And so, we pass these on to you.

&

'Verse, Chorus'

I've been going to the Heath to cruise with the parakeets. Feral, swooping as they sense the coming on, a little later every day, of sunset. A greener green than even the newish limeish leaves. That spring feeling: that red teardrop on the map: we are here.

How did the parakeets get here, a zillion miles from their tropical habitat? Some say the first were Jimi Hendrix's, set free, a grace note. I remember reading about the feral flocks of Telegraph Hill, San Francisco, in Armistead Maupin's *Tales of the City*. Maybe they're in queer communion, what trends there slowly soughing here. The green of the rainbow.

You can't cruise a parakeet though, because no human knows what their love language is. I mean, you're meant to steer clear of them, H5N1n.iii. They're meant to be dead, but then so am I. It's harder and harder to get the antiretrovirals now, how retro. So, we keep our distance, measured in song. I cruise with them. Put on my best drag and sync my lips to their beaks. On wing, singing and dancing, all flash and glory with their forked tails.

There's a song, many songs, in which birds carry word of

a murder back to the murdered person's lover, or mother. In 'The Three Ravens' (Child 26), the birds cannot get near the slain knight because his hawks and hounds are so loyal. But less noble soldiers who lack an entourage may call the birds to them at the point of death, a living being to be with them.

Corvids, mostly, birds of Odin and scavenge and prophecy. Crows are busy in this plague season. Gathering like thrown ashes on the clipped lawns of gated, estated politicians to make our banned protests. Leaving the Tower together, clipped wings supporting each other over the walls and electrified fences. Let it fall.

What do parakeets carry? Seeds of.

Go tell my lovers who live too far to cycle here, some now on the other side from which there is no … yes. Tell that I'm dancing for them, up against the rough bark that has kissed their skins. It's spring and in the midst of so much death the sap is rising. A little earlier each year. And the birds, the birds are singing.

&

'High Note'

You'd have to be a hare to get all the way up Cadair Idris, and then, boom, you'd be got by a red kite or kestrel or peregrine falcon. They've come back, the board in the carapark says. We hear blackbirds and thrushes, but they say the thing with birds of prey is you don't see them till they're on you.

SO MAYER

Being young and full of spunk, we started climbing in our trainers, just as a way to get away from our families. We didn't get even close to Penygader, distracted by all the things that two young leverets can play at in a giant's chair. Look, there's the caravan, fuck, isn't it tiny? Down there at the start of Tŷ Nant, the Pony Path, in the carapark, resting on its shafts. Shafts, hahahah. Pony, hahaha. Bareback. Want one of these? Want some of this? Fuck yes. Friskin and foolin.

Somehow we made it as far as the iron gate where the Gwynant crosses the path and we drank from it, although you're not supposed to – even this high up there's forever chemicals. Then we sat sleepy with our backs against the warm stone wall, chatting this and that. The roads we've been on, the horse fair coming up, the jokes of it that after the Pox – our mas call it the PCSC Act but pfffft – tried to eliminate us, we're all this place has got right now for moving stuff from pillar to post on the roads. The only ones who can cross the border between the old enemies. No more gas, no more oil, not even chip fat. They're working on ethanol, but some fuckers keep stealing it and drinking it, haha. So, we're the postal service, the delivery service, lots of nice help yourself and hello missus. I'm into it, but he's not. Don't let them stick me between the shafts and serve them, he says. Shaft, hahaha, and then we're at each other's flies again. It's hot up here.

We don't know that down in the valley, they've took guns to go hunting.

When we wake up burned and thirsty, we drink some more of the weird water. The sun is dipping goldenred, goldenrod. Did you dream you were a fish? he asks me, and leaps in to skinny dip just as the sun does. Flash of arse muscle clenching as he hits the cold. Yeah, I say. Undress and dive after.

&

'In the Wings'

The beavers are building a lil theatre. Thanks, Nature. The day we get news that the council's shut down Black Boxxx at CLAY. No more stage shows & sex shows & club nights & late nights & workshops & swap shops for queer & trans fam in this neck of the treeless woods, txxx.

We spent years building up that place after the so-called Broken Promise Riots, the righteous protests against the sell-off of England's freeports to private off-planet investors, which spread ofcourse inland, because rivers connect us to the sea. Even us, smack dab in the middle. Even the Aire gets there eventually, squeezing into the Ouse as the Ouse oozes out into the Humber. All the glass and ironwork of our arcades turned into a living video game, must-have smash and grabs by the scared middle classes before escaping to their Airbnbs in the countryside.

We stayed, like clay. This is gritstone moor country. We don't run. We show roots. From the broken promise, Black Boxxx. And, after ten years, it's gone. Like all my fingernails. I lay my toolbelt down, defeated. We've been moved on because the neighbours complained. Our all-gender, 24/7 toilet was

SO MAYER

'illegal and wasteful, a lightning rod for trouble'. Which they know how?, being that they're an off-planet conglomerate running an automated warehouse. That wants our lil space, probs to house a generator for more surveillance.

So, I watch beaver cam and work my cuticles. It's called a mani*cure*. It's not sulking – it's rewilding. Fine. It's both. I'm non-binary: that means I can keep one eye on the screen and one on the orange stick, right. This cam's from somewhere called Ealing. Leafy burbs and all that. Fantasy. But look at the beavers, they're the ultimate stage managers, hot butches with everything in their toolbox, teeth and tail and claws. Rrrrrrr. That sleek and gap-tooth look of the eighties dyke spoken-word poet in my great-aunt's pics. Dam, girl.

In my dreams, sweetly herbed, I stroke the fur of the down-south beaver and tell her about the show we were gna do. *Twenty Questions for Vesta*. Time past that Tilley, Britain's foremost male impersonator (billed as) was better known. Time past she answered for herself.

Where did you get that hat, Vesta, and was it from marrying a Tory MP?

How you feel, Vesta, recruiting all those young soldiers to die in a colonial war?

But also, Tilley, spill the real tea. Did you ever go see Gladys Bentley over the sea? How it feels to wear that suit in front of all those stuffed shirts who think they're laughing at you when you're laughing at them? How did it feel to come up on the stage, from hardscrabble to high society? Are you ever not putting on the Ritz? What's a Ritz?

TRUTH & DARE

In reality, I watch the viewing numbers fluctuate, wondering if it's all off-planet bots or if any other Boxxxers are randomly watching. I send them links then switch to silent. Do not disturb. Protest mode, untraceable. I'm not ready to talk yet. I'm still sitting on the folding chair, on the beanbag, leaning against my friend's wheelchair, waiting bated for the show to start.

Look, I want to tap. The beaver dam has wings now, a revolve. Up in the flies, vines tangle. It's beautiful. Wilding, no re-.

On the boards, a heron and a cormorant face off, or dance, a complex chorus line flashed through by a kingfisher bling as, classic MC. But after the sapphire flash, here's the grey morning suit versus top hat and tux. Doing the Lambent Walk.

OK, I tap, I'm ready to talk.

&

'Plan B'

The funny thing is that getting the morning-after pill the first day of a zombie apocalypse is really no easier or harder than on a previously average day. No bigger a deal, the obstacles are just ... different. More slow-moving brain-eating hordes, sure, but fewer overtly religiose or obstructive pharmacists. The baseball bat I brought to use in case of the former was also effective on the triple-lock cabinets erected by the latter. The very last packet, anywhere in ends. I know 'cause I've looked. I scoop some antiseptic wipes and cream, coco-d's, other stuff for the other stuff. Sure, there are no prescription forms to complete, but most of the bottled water is gone. Hard to swallow.

Still, it's always been make do and mend for us. For us, the A in the circle has long stood for abortion as well as anarchism: what's more basic to self-governance and autonomy than deciding whether to incubate another life in your body? In the before times, we had time to read Emma Goldman and Rosa Luxemburg and Alexandra Kollontai on the centrality of reproductive justice to the formation of Eurowestern anarchism. Super-kosher of them: abortion rights are right there in rabbi stuff. My mums' Judaism went as far as, and no further than, having a poster of the Ruttenberg Accords that had legalised free, safe and accessible global abortion when they were teenagers. Not that they were liberals, fuck no. I come by my anarchism natural.

In the before times, though, I'd have been stealing T, not B, and HRT for my sweet girl C. Alone among hormonals, levonorgestrel seems to have survived the second war (just), and so has Viagra, but gender-affirmative pharmaceuticals, forget it. Banned to the eye teeth, even for cis people who need them. Just in case they give them to us.

So here I am, on the morning after, proudly carrying out what Emma and Rosa and Alexandra and millions of others fought for: baseball bats for bodily autonomy. The only problem now is: how do I find a space to stay still and safe enough to take pills that make me vomit and shake, when I'm

TRUTH & DARE

caught between zombie hordes and human mobs? Because waking up in the aftermath, without Cecilia *who is never not there*, and among the soldiers who've come out of nowhere and aren't going anywhere, I can't go back to bed. Not now, not ever.

I take shelter in the remains of a bus shelter, not that it offered much when it was erect with its evil backless, too-high, hard plastic non-bench of hate. Even the zombies are avoiding it, and the slow crunch-crunch of smashed safety glass that gives their shuffle away. I'm about to pop and dry swallow when this fox comes up to me. Right up to my feet in their duct-taped vegan boots. And in its mouth is a dead pigeon, its entrails as red as the plastic I'm slipping off. And, no shit, it sets the pigeon down at my feet, crosses its little black front paws and bows, then trots away. Over the sensation of trying not to puke, I clock that I'm equal parts honoured and yacked out, and clock that, woah, this is genuinely a feeling I've never had before. First time for so much, these days.

And as if that wasn't enough, I'd almost got fully down the High when this man swathed in a massive long black coat, the kind you can hide three kids inside and still carry your life in its pockets, swings out and says, 'Hand it over.' Or maybe 'Stand and deliver.' He's got a black N95 on, as well as goggles and a hat, and it's hard to make anything out over the automated government warning sirens going off on all the zombies' phones. But I can't lose this little packet carried in my hand. Better to lose my life right now than to carry a life I just can't.

So, I pull down my own bandanna and roar and swing my baseball bat out, flickering images of a yellow fringed dress and the smash of glass. No joke, he jumps back, starts shaking. And after a stumbled beat, I realise it's with laughter. I realise it's my love.

Fucking Sovay, my C. Riding out before I was awake, disguised in my clothes despite how boy mode makes her feel as sick as girl mode makes me, planning on stealing a pill from the first person she saw on the street. For me.

A gallon jug of liberated water in one hand, with the other she scoops me up and takes me to this warehouse that's, for the moment, our home, where I swallow and swoon. As we passed the bus stop, though, where no bus will ever stop again, I swear I saw a pigeon fly up and out, entrails as red as a fox, as red as the fires.

&

'Shanty'

So, obvs, we've become pirates.

Temporary autonomy, rum and sodomy, really great ripped up shirts from Traid, all that. On the canals we hand round our spoils, a floating food etc bank where you need no proof. Shopping trolleys grow natural in water: we fish 'em out, fill 'em up with tins and tampons and things we've liberated. Food wants to be free and who are we to stand in its way? So, we flow.

The navigations out of Gas Street Basin are no longer bustling, but bristling. Which is good for us, giving us cover and shade to throw. A canal boat is slow, but a coracle is quick. Canoes zoom. There's private security, prisecs (aka pricks, because what else?), but given the pricks are landlubbers, all they can do is dronebomb us.

Come on. Every man Jack among us can hack. And when we say 'Jack', we mean us in our short jacket and white trousers, like Shirley and Dolly Collins sang, we mean when Jack went a-sailing. All the old songs might claim it's a put-on, a sailor's suit supposedly unsuited to a body that curves differently, and we'll be back in skirts when we hit land. *We* aren't cosplaying pirates, in either sense. We've been torrenting since we were old enough to flip off parental controls. So now we have a fleet of anarcho-drones that deliver up and over the crumbly inaccessible canal side. Anything you can make, we can make better.

And of late we hear rumours there's people shoring up the ruins to make stable places to sit and drink, to ride a repaired bike, to push a pushchair. They say it happens at night and, well, there's no electrics anymore. We like that. Navigate by the stars, haha, canals are all straight lines and fucked locks. But one night, while we're unfucking a stuck lock, running behind what we call our schedule, something heartskipping flicks the corners of our eyes. Is that? Was that? Just the mass of buddleja bobbing its purple packers.

At ease. During the day we'd gathered spicy heartsease, *Viola tricolor*, from hanging baskets gone to seed like everything in the Mudlands' town centres, trailing down low to the cracked rainbow crosswalks. Talk about civic

Pride. High streets are for weeds. Pirates need greens. We are sensitive to the rustling of leaves and rising scents and—

Fuck shirts, they have cloaks. Move with a boundless grace over rubble and slabs. Humming. It's the humming that gets us. Lulls us in our hammocks so we drift, touching, a tender coming into sleep. Feels the weirdest thing: safe.

In the pre-dawn, a single feather left on the smooth, strong mud and twig of the banks. We see: glistening jars of bramble jelly, bundles of railway track rosemary, baskets and baskets of wild garlic from the roadsides. Green and green and gold. We load up, leaves releasing their sharp, necessary resins on our fingertips and in our nostrils.

Once we're done, there's a single fisherperson sat sound, nested almost, nodding to us over a dandelion root coffee. Steam rising. They offer but we wave it off. It's tea for the tillerman, herbs drunk to a mulch we read and use for tilaks. Deep green. We offload boxes for them to pass on, a nosegay of heartsease atop each as thanks, and we cast off, slowly, looking back for.

Our foraging albatrosses, we think. Loving them. Literally shipping. Our fix-it sirens, burd gurls. Our flag means life, ongoing: a gull wing, grey and wide against the wide, grey sky.

&

'Refrain'

I hated it here, at first. I'm from the city. Well, Hastings is I suppose a town. But you know, at least it has tings. Or had. Before it fell in the sea. It was white enough there and it's whiter here. Whiteness everywhere. And not just because I'm a shepherd.

Shepherdess, I guess. Rhymes with tress, dress, confess, less. Everything femme about me but my piercing whistle. The farm folk are fine enough, having been saddled with yet another land girl who has fuck-all idea how to saddle a thing. Up Shit Hill without a sandal.

They're a bit biblical, which, when there's been floods and that, what can you expect? But like literal, with the beards and woollen robes and hemp rope sandals, and yes, Sussex is kind of a desert, and yes, I take my sheep to the well. At least there's flatbread and cheese and herbs.

And yes, I guess, as of yesterday: kissing cousins. That's what we call each other at the farm, all the youngers. 'Cousin' this and 'cousin' that. 'Sister' and 'brother' are only for the ones born to it. Bully for them which, yeah, there's bullying.

She gets it worse, worse than me, for being mixed, which they call an abomination. Light-skinned and green-eyed and freckled, as her hair grew out of its twists they shaved it, again and again. Come just this winter from the Sodom that was Brighton. Three full moon nights I've lain awake to count her brilliant piercings like the lost constellations hidden behind satellites, sighing with desire for her. Sometimes she's let me rub lanolin on her bruises.

Nowruz, right?, she said, this dawn, as we walked the sheep up from Caburn Bottom, offering me an egg. Not painted or anything, but AN EGG. We're not let near the chicken sheds, but she's a thief of genius. It's only late March but the old fort stones up on Mount Caburn are hot enough that, with a stick, a bit of patience, and a bit of wild marjoram she picked on the way up, we can mostly scramble it.

She scoops a warm handful into my mouth, her fingers slippy with albumen. I – do I? – dare to do the same. We suck at each other's fingers, both flashing on lambs. Our life is lambs atm, spring etc. When we're separated and shying a bit (or I am), I say, It's near shearing season. Last year was my first and it was …

We meet each other's gaze, her greeny eyes matching the day-old bruise on her chin.

Like that, yeah.

Yeah.

Show me so I know what I'm doing.

What?

Look, you be the sheep.

So, I show her how to hold me with her thighs, her fingers free to slide herb and yolk through all my length of hair to tingle my scalp. Again, in fistfuls. I wriggle at the feeling, and that's when it happens. Kissing. Her tongue stud. Her fingers lifting my smock, thighs holding my thigh.

We take the long way home, me whistling through the late dusk, her brushing the chalk from the back of my robe. Shivers. Night falls faster and blowier than we expect and, lost as the flock is, we take shelter in an abandoned house, standing alone in the lee of the chalk ridge. Maybe a seer lived here once, she says, touching the faded tapestries woven through with words, the strange instruments with their long necks. We could stay here, I say.

We sleep, and – limbs to limbs – do not sleep, then sleep. And when I wake sharp and long before dawn, there is no house, and the dew is a glimmer on her beautiful face, and in the sky a winged shadow lifts, Simurgh, its voice singing like the last of starlight: 'for I am thine and thou art mine, no man shall uncomfort thee'.

First light, we can see the farmhouse is somehow just over the next field. We find our lambs close by, alive, their tight new wool warm against our hands. Maybe it will be OK.

&

'To the Beat'

We're a lot of Pollies Oliver here. Some of us are Pollies under the combats, and some of us are Olivers forever. 'Like in that fairy tale, *Monstrous Regiment*,' one of us says. 'I remember my great-grandda telling that one to me, and then retelling it, a bit every night, what can be remembered.' None of us is trolls or vampires or blouses or English, at least not yet because you can turn into anything these days, but we all have our reasons for being here. There's food, such as it is, which is mainly booze we brew out of rotten potatoes. But it's safe to fuck. When there's not raids.

In the song, there's a doctor, which is something like a magician. Magicians across the sea are what started this war, with all their turning soil into oil, so we're not sure about going back to doctoring. We scratch our itches and wash our wounds with spit. We make poultices out of seaweed, there's one of us crossed over from Muff who knows how. Yesterday, we found enough tree branches, and sturdy enough – sessile oak, not the English kind – and we made new crutches. So now we're all back on foot, marching with our arms, and ready for it, whatever comes: our day, or something otherwise.

What come are doves, these small white drones, which means peace if we trust it, and that means the end of food and booze and us. Polly Oliver, she has to go home with her captain. We haven't heard the end of the story yet. 'Oh, there's always another war,' the teller says. We're not sure about going back, and we're not sure about going back to that.

&

'Solo'

On the marsh under RAF Forres, no planes in sight, just swans the size of planes.

Mending nets to fish for dinner, I think about nettles. Nettle shirts. How so many of us are half-boy, half-swan, one arm and one wing. How many of us have blisters on our hands from sewing to save our brothers, to salve our sisters.

Swan is *Cygnus*, almost sing-us. My grandmothers used to sing and sign for me 'The Bonny Swans', about one sister who kills another out of jealousy. You'd think I long for a sister, alone here. But there's so much to see.

TRUTH & DARE

At sunset there's a scintillant moment when a bird, or maybe a cloud, seems to step out of the sky and speak with its wing-fingers. But I turn my head away, blinking back tears of light. I – hand raised from chest to chin – suffice.

&

'Fine'

You come back, and here I am. Stood on stone. Stone myself, berry-brown and lichened. I have dyed so many times.

Whose, you say, and I say, No man.

You have come back as you do with every wheel of the year, being migratory.

Time and time again, spring comes. Even after we wrecked the seasons. And here it is again, and I am budding. Polyping. You look at my volva but can't see, yet, the deep mycelium.

Where is it, this Winsbury? you ask, your boat in my cove. Here, I say. Now. It's how we win. Together.

zeus

The first time I saw God I was eight years old.

&

In a dark wood, I had strayed from the path.
It wasn't exactly a wood, and I was still on the gravel, but the night was dark and tree-filled and I was hopelessly lost and scared, and the wind was in the leaves, in the roaring sky, above me.
I was running – had been running, full tilt, tilting (that is) into hypoxia, a result of the combination of complete and absolute terror and being born prematurely, with both under-developed lungs and asthma.
So, take this story with a pinch of potential brain function impairment.

&

Not this bit though: we were playing Holocaust.
I was at a Jewish summer camp for two weeks, in a rambling

old boarding school somewhere in East Sussex, near Bexhill. The adult supervisors were having a night off, and we had been left in the charge of the teenage counsellors (who, at nineteen, seemed impossibly grown-up and sophisticated to me).

We'd roasted vegetarian sausages and baked potatoes around an immense bonfire in one of the back fields of the school, and been given our share of Jewish ghost stories by its lurid light: the golem of Prague, the dybbuk.

And then it was time to run.

We were (playing, although at eight the distinction is not strict, and anyway, how is this play?) Jews in the Warsaw Ghetto Uprising, the counsellors (dressed in black and carrying – I think – rounders bats) were Nazis rounding us up. We were split into small groups, and told we had to make it back into the school, to a specific classroom where the ghost stories would be finished. There we would be safe – but the main and side doors were patrolled by other counsellors, who were on the lookout to catch us.

If we were caught ... Threat, and a rounders bat, and history, hang in the air.

&

I'd been separated, in headlong flight, from my group of temporary friends, and found myself with two older campers I didn't really know. They were maybe fourteen or fifteen, not much younger than the counsellors but far older than me in that way teenagers are – yet as terrified as we primary school kids were. A girl and a boy.

We were running past tall hedges overtopped by summer-crowned oak trees with leaves like dark, reaching hands, down a gravel path that the boy thought for sure led to the school. The girl, fleet and tall, was running ahead, whispering fiercely back to us to keep up.

And then she wasn't.

She was on the ground, pale and still.

Her boyfriend took off to 'get help', leaving me – a pre-teen – alone in the dark with an unconscious person. She had run straight into the steel arm that barred the path (which was, of course, the school's driveway) to cars, and gone down hard, backwards. She was still breathing. She was bleeding. I covered her with my terrible grey coat, which I loved and my mother hated, a factory second from a friend of my parents who was (their term) a schmatte merchant.

It was a typical English August, cold and damp and fierce with wind.

It was Warsaw in 1943. It was sixteenth-century Prague. It was York, 1190. It was the Pale, on fire, again and again.

It was timeless, suspended in terror: night, cold words of prayer.

&

Shema Yisrael, Adonai Eloheinu, Adonai Echad.
Hear, O Israel, the Lord is our God, the Lord is One.

TRUTH & DARE

It's the first prayer that a Jewish child learns, a credo much like the Lord's Prayer or the Shahada.

Said daily in synagogue, it is also the prayer that one is supposed to use to call on God in a time of need – which is odd, because it addresses Israel (the global and historical Jewish community), not God.

Words given to the dark, one by one, on short, burning bursts of breath.

&

> My ultra-Orthodox Jewish parents called God Hashem, meaning 'the Name'. Even the appellation Adonai, 'my master,' was too sacred for them to utter in casual conversation, let alone God's true name: the tetragrammaton, Yehava [more usually transliterated as Yahweh]. In Jewish legend, the golem, a man of clay, was animated by a paper in his mouth that bore this secret name of God. I've come to think of the great ossified colossus of their faith as animated in the same way.
>
> — Jericho Vincent, 'How to Digest Sludge'

I haven't said the Shema in three decades. When I wake from recurrent nightmares (in which I am not infrequently Anne Frank, although no one else knows or believes me), it no longer springs to my tongue, defence against the dark.

But I remember it, with the deep muscle memory of

childhood repetition in synagogue and Hebrew school and dark bedrooms. Training – now I look back – for holy war. Religious instruction *is* the apocalypse it so desperately wants to take place, and children are, mercilessly, its victims.

&

That night, when God came towards me out of the darkness, or of the darkness, what I saw was light: bright silver, slender, a blazing gap in the world that resolved itself into the helmed figure of Joan of Arc.

&

I have never, until now, told anyone that I'd seen God in the person of a French teenage girl/warrior/witch.

But I remember it.

I don't remember what happened to the girl who ran into the pole (although I remember her being alive and fine in the days that followed), or what happened to my coat, or how I got back into the school. I remember crouching under a desk in the desiccated classroom, where I heard a version of the story of Rabbi Judah Loew and his golem.

I don't remember the story, but I remember the stone-mouth sensation of holding a word silent in my mouth, as the golem was said to do.

&

TRUTH & DARE

In the middle of the night, sometime between 3 and 4 August 1981, I cried out.

I was three and very almost a half, and I had gone to the toilet, more or less in my sleep. And now I was stuck.

I cried out, and my mother didn't come. She was (although I hadn't quite understood this) in hospital, giving birth to brother one (of two).

There is no heroic end to this story: God did not answer my prayer, and nor did I. I did not learn resilience, or self-sufficiency, or even some elementary physics (leverage, gravity). I cried out, and my father came for me.

&

When Will Shagsberd says that 'As flies to wanton boys are we to th' gods,' he comes close to the truth (sorry Wills, no cigar).

There are no gods.

There are only the wanton boys within us all. Terrified by their want – by the fact that they, too, have cried out in need – they set out to destroy ([that which reminds them of that want in] themselves).

&

> Shevek saw that he had touched in these men an impersonal animosity that went very deep. Apparently they, like the tables on the ship, contained a woman,

a suppressed, silenced, bestialized woman, a fury in a cage.

— Ursula K Le Guin, *The Dispossessed*

&

Shevek is an anarchist, returned to the planet that his revolutionary ancestors left, from the hardscrabble moon where he lives in a society of (and requiring, in order to function on minimal resources) full gender equality. The men he's talking to are capitalists and socialists and scientists, both conservative and liberal, and they share a gendered belief system that is still familiar to us.

How the men in *The Dispossessed* (and incels and others of the alt right) fear the specific fury that they have made by caging their imagined woman within themselves. How much they want her to emerge and – sword between her couture-swathed shoulder blades – punish them, deliciously.

Bored, now.

&

My favourite story about a god, who is often depicted as a woman warrior although she has a complex gender identity, is this:

> When still a little girl, sitting upon her father's knees, [Artemis] spoke in this childish way to her father: 'Gimme

virginity, Daddy, to preserve forever, and to be called by many names, so that Phoebus may not rival me. And gimme arrows and bows ... and [let me] be a light-bearer and ... hitch up my tunic with a fringed border as far as my knees, so that I may kill wild beasts ... Gimme all the mountains, and any city, whichever you wish. For it is rare when Artemis will go down to a town. I'll dwell in the mountains.'

— Callimachus, 'Hymn to Artemis', translated by Susan A Stephens

This is no war-machine-endorsing Diana Prince.

Hitching her tunic (a non-gendered garment) to her knees, Artemis refuses the grown-up pudicity of ankle-skimming classical Athenian women's dress. It's a tomboy call that resonates still.

Susan A Stephens' cheeky use of 'gimme' for Callimachus's slangy 'dos' is not incidental. What Artemis gives, especially to young women, is shelter. Her 'virginity' is something other than (more than) what we think of: it is to not be defined (as women otherwise were) by the sexual. It is asulon (from which comes: asylum), inviolability. It is not a cage, but its opposite.

Gimme freedom.

&

Gods don't seem much different to me than poltergeists, although inversely: a child, terrified by their vulnerability, imagines the adult they feel (and fear) they have to become.

Vengeful, it seems. All-powerful, with that saccharine Mary Poppins spoonful of mercy that is another form of absolute sway, in always demanding abject gratitude.

We get the gods that, culturally, we deserve, and so Eurowestern cisheteropatriarchal colonial capitalism scares itself with a white male thunderer made in its impotent wish-fear image.

&

What stepped out of the darkness, to me, as Jeanne la Pucelle, no longer silenced or bestialised – and why? [She] was the leader of the French resistance, condemned to death (as Marina Warner argues in *Alone of All [Her] Sex*, reading court transcripts) for [her] Artemisian sartorial, physical, and intellectual gender transgression.

Although [she] was imprisoned, [she] remained eloquent and self-confident until the end, whether talking to [her] judges or [her] confessor.

Jean/ne is neither #GirlBoss nor patriarchy's erotic fantasy of revenge. [She] is asulon, inviolability. A figure of possibility, unossifying.

&

In a moment of deep fear – fear for my life, for another's life – perhaps what I found (rushing wind; fitful moonlight) was, conversely, freedom.

Not perversely: I wasn't getting off on the thrill of the drama, or wallowing in an operatic death wish. I cried out to the night because, in feeling this specific, utterly embodied, identifiable, and immediate fear, I was strangely set free from (and simultaneously aware of) the constant, unnameable dread I had lived as my everyday.

Because here I was kneeling by irrefutable evidence of the violence that fear could do, of what domination drove people to. Breathless, yes, but I could bear witness.

Hear, O Israel, the Lord is our God, the Lord is One – and the Lord didn't do shit to stop this.

I owe him no allegiance. His existence is no longer a philosophical issue, it's moot. It (and he) matters not a jot, not a tittle.

What matters here is this: wind, this night, this body. This girl, these girls, a word that, historically, means a child of any gender. This ground, of everything.

&

We have expended so much of our human energy on making gods, and then making those gods' wars, inside, as much as outside, us. And then on fighting the gods we created, denying them, destroying them. And telling all three of those stories – creating, fighting, destroying – as heroic narratives.

What could we do, other-wise, wise to other possibilities, with that energy? People love Sara Ahmed's phrase FEMINIST

KILLJOY, and it does look good on a glitter necklace, but they don't often listen for what may not fit on the necklace, but comes next: 'killing joy is a world-making project'.

&

By which I do not mean, 'Be a god.' If we unmake the gods, we need to unmake them in ourselves, most of all.

What would it look like, as a human, to take part in the slow project of making a world? Re-reading *The Dispossessed*, I see it would look like hard fucking never-ending work. I've spent years trying to make – recycle, salvage, filter, detoxify, live in the ruins of – one single human self, and that's been hard enough.

But then I remember: we are already working all the time, expending everything we are just to uphold the toxic apocalyptic godhead. Working in and being worked by our Eurowestern culture(s), our institutions, even our language. No wonder we are all so tired all the time.

Time to stop. To rest, to believe there is the rest – the more that must be possible. To fall to our knees and be. Vulnerable, inviolable: there is no contradiction.

&

When I stopped running, when I fell into the classic pose of supplication (not a Jewish one, but I'd read my Greek myths and knew how to Thetis it when necessary), when I let myself cry out, give sound to my need and fear, it was not God who came to me.

It was a girl like me. Like I didn't know I could be.

They bore no lightning because they were the lightning.

They had no destruction to offer, nor any resurrection. No promise to make, no sacrifice to take. Nothing but to bear witness, with me, to injury and to fear, and – despite them, within them – to our continued existence, in relation to each other, in the face of violence and domination.

Persistence, a fact of being. In the world, breath by ragged breath. We were. We are.

Keeping. Going.

Dune Elegies

Here, at the end of all things.

A cuspate foreland is a place of sharp angles, ridged dunes formed over five millennia by longshore drift moving sediment in opposing directions. Elegy or genesis, they are one and the same. Watching something end is remembering its beginning. You can't be sentimental here; the wind is too sharp and the shingle won't let you sleep. Time is too dense, held in quartzite lattices, like revenge.

If you let yourself, if you were less worried about breaking an HRT-less bone grown brittle, you could chip axeheads, arrowheads, from the flint. You know your history: the Happisburgh hand axe found two hundred miles north up the coast, dropped or lost there 500,000 years ago, in Doggerland. Leaf-shaped, diamond-shaped, a thing of great beauty with its shirred and smoky facets ridged like dunes. From the same beach, you can see the wreck of *HMS Dungeness*, covered in sand since it was bombstruck in 1940.

Sand is stone, you know that. Sandy beaches were once shingle. You could see attrition as violence, or as patience. Sand is what happens when the answer to every question is 'not yet'. It's loss, micaceous. It's gone, when gone is often where you need to be. No tears, just sand in your eye. Don't call it crying. It's the wind.

In spring, bitterns boom from the wildflower meadows, nesting near the lakes, away from the exposed shore. Turn your face hard up to the sky, a concrete listening mirror. Lade is the only place on the isles that all three mirror models were installed, and all were obsolete before the aircraft, laden with bombs, passed overhead.

This is a listening place. That's why you came here. The dilapidated planks of Marconi's wireless shed, where it all began: the sending of messages over airwaves. He crossed the channel without moving. The stones still resonate with the words he sent. Stone does not give up easily. Now it radiates tritium leaked from the power plant, so few others come here. Once there was radar here, erected by Decca Navigation. Yes, that Decca, the OG British record company, although they sold off their war business after WWII to Northrop Grumman. Thanks, chaps.

Where there is listening, there is surveillance. Where there is space, there is the military. You came here to get away, to find the peace between desire and technology at the end of the fossil fuel era, but there is no getting away. Where there are lighthouses, there are foghorns, or the echo of them. The Experimental Station holds a test structure, although it's now privatised, designer postmodernist architecture. Bitterns boo from the meadows.

Or they used to. In the late spring, you would find

eggshells that you made into headphones with a little twist of copper wire. Now there are no more swifts or sand martins, swallows, wheatears, or black redstarts. There may still be warblers migrating, but not through here.

The autumn of the world is permanent, all wither and no harvest. *The sedge is withered from the lake*, you think, *and no birds sing*.

You have had many names, so many that you are plural, like the shingle (have you ever seen a single shing?). La Belle Dame sans Merci, sure, that's one of them, popular among your long-ago exes. Kisses four? As if that's enough. Bye, bushes. The Margravine of the Marshes, that's your favourite. When you were no longer allowed to play on, terfed off your own radio show after you transitioned, you came here, with your van full of vinyl that you were slowly digitising.

You sat – well, squatted – in the lighthouse, letting your sounds play out, still reeling out your midnight introductions, but now not broadcasting but podcasting. Strange phrase. You think of pods of marine mammals entangled in cast nets, fishing no longer like when the beach was lined with dinghies down from the Pilot Inn. You used to see seals sunning themselves on the shingle, squat and alert like the tanning coppers where the nets were treated with resin. Resinant. That could be another of your names.

What is a listening mirror? You understand the science of it, of course you do, but the decision to call it a mirror. In your recording studio at the top of the lighthouse, you always face the window, face the way it blurs the soft lines that now undefine your face, the way your skin makes waves as it is loosening from your bones. You are not looking at your face, though, but through it, through the window, as if there will be an engineer on the other side, as you once had been before you found your voice as a DJ. As if there will be a listener, hovering in the noctilucent reflection where gulls used to float. You send out sounds, not knowing if there are still ears to listen. It's been years since the trains ran, or the diesel buses. You don't have a car because there are no charging points. Your solar-power credits go towards hot water, your music, your casts.

In the absence of birds, you find yourself playing birdsong between the tracks, lining up Screamin' Jay Hawkins and the whisper-song of blue jays. The spell palls, leaves you sad. Even Natacha Atlas's cover, orchestrated like a Soad Hosny film, can't save you in its euphoria. Not even Queen Latifah's smoky voice so close in the mix. Not even queen Nina. Nah nah nah nah nah. You sometimes just sit sipping your desalinated, chloriney water – you have to purify your own – and wonder what it means to be queer here, all alone. When the birds were calling, you felt closer to yourself, like there was an indirect link between your life in flight and their throats, their wings, their fragile egglife, even their nests, however cisheteronormative almost every nature documentary makes them out to be.

You think about the legendary documentary you once saw, did someone send you a code or a rip, a silent film – although they'd added a piano score (they, the restorer, which was a museum, you think). The film was a strange hybrid beast, aren't we all, darling, part old-school nature documentary, mostly shot in labs or farms or other human-interfered-with environments because it was from, what, the twenties? The thirties? It doesn't matter, it's all ancient history now, so last century, like you are.

The other half of the film was even older. Felt old, static in some ways, its one-shot set-ups and monochromatic make-up and melodramatic acting. You once searched to see whether the story being re-enacted was in fact true, but you fell down a well of facts about the actor playing the gay pianist who may or may not have been based on a real person. He was the actor whom everyone would remember as the German major in *Casablanca*, although he was a Jew, or perhaps he said he was a Jew because he opposed the Nazis. Something Conrad, was that his name, like the seafaring novelist. You are haunted by something he said in an interview in 1941, haunted even more after reading that his daughter found out about his death from a radio broadcast: 'If you believe in waves, which you must believe after you have the radio, why couldn't human beings contact the wave lengths of someone who is dead?'

After you have the radio. It's that *after*, like radio called the dead into. You think about that as you brood over your homebrew water, cuing up your next track: Moor Mother's 'Nighthawk of Time (feat Black Quantum Futurism)'. Shit, it's only seventy-three seconds, you don't have much time – it flies through time with a scream. You wonder if you are broadcasting to the dead. You remember Conrad's yearning

TRUTH & DARE

face in the dying moments of the old film, as he takes an overdose because taking the blackmailer to court has made his sexuality public, and now he is ostracised from making music. Touché. But that's not the end of the film, wait. You cue up 'embrace' from Kìzis' *The Palm of My Nature*, a blissful twenty-four minutes, twenty-five secs of listening, let it be present, try not to be hungry. Kisses four. Goddamn. That's what the film is about, the old documentary, it's called *Laws of Love*, as in 'birds do it, bees do it'. Maybe it was released around the same time as the song, although you prefer 'Let's Misbehave', of course you do, the original song Cole Porter wrote for *Paris*, for its rhyming of camels and mammals, a childhood feverdream memory of the extraordinary dance sequence to it in *Pennies from Heaven* (American version), shouldn't all musicals be watched in a fever dream?

Breathe. This is how your mind is now, looped like tangled 1/8-inch tape that used to festoon every bush of greater knapweed or rarer lizard orchid rewilding the 500,000 kilometres of road verges that loop around the UK, this is how your mind was driving then, how it always was if you're honest. Your infamous monologues weaving together songs and their stories, sound *tracks*. Back to that silent film with its tinkling piano score. There are birds and bees, and dancing mice, all in pairs and pairs until it comes to the insect world, the plant world, what is happening? Caterpillars into cocoons then releasing gauzy wings. Flowers that fertilise themselves. You relaxed into it, laughed when a section hymning motherhood cut from an overdone Renaissance Mary breastfeeding Jesus to the intertitle: Intersexuals. This was the real material, the reason that no one knew about the film, because it had been banned – no, burned – the reason it had been restored, the reason your friend had sent you the link to watch late at night lazily in bed with your then-ex at a time when you assumed that would be a thing forever.

Reason is the film's guiding light, if you remember. Science will triumph, justice will prevail, the laws of nature include species diversity and intraspecies diversity, we are birds and we are bees, watch us sing and dance. You remember feeling a little bitter, because you know your history: this kind-eyed man with the moustache, this man delivering the lecture that frames the documentary material, is a man who would have understood you. A closeted gay German-Jewish doctor who dedicated his life to ending the laws against sodomy, including by making films. How much time he spent arguing with people who didn't listen to him (is that your bitterness?), only to die in exile. You decide to end the show with Arooj Aftab's 'Ovid's Metamorphoses', for Ovid's own exile was caused by (in his words), 'carmen et error', a song – or a spell – and a mistake. Aftab's track is an ambient hymn to what must have been bird islands off some rocky Mediterranean cliff, the poet's Sirenum Scopuli, *Siren Lookouts* (title of the album). You have to be up high to find your listeners, to send out your sound, you know that.

You watch the timer tick down through Aftab's fifteen mins, eleven secs of analogue synthesiser loops, delays, and reverbs swirling like whirlpools under her seavoice, all recorded live and tracked to a single mono input for that siren's-throat feeling, pouring out, calling. You respond, aroused by the opening in her voice. While the recording renders, then buffers, before casting, you feel yourself, your hand a seashell, your heat building like a wave, waves, sound waves that echo, as the song plays again around you from your speaker stacks, your siren lookouts with their pulsing throats. Oh.

Making dinner – a rehydrated packet of Soylent and pickled sea kale from your cache sunk into the shingle – you decide you miss the birds more than your lovers. Two solar credits to heat the Soylent, all the nutrients you need; you hate it, as if you didn't live on speed and protein shakes when you were engineering. You remember dragging your then-lover, and sometimes-engineer, on a pilgrimage with you when you read that the actor – Conrad something, Violet, maybe? – was in the columbarium at the Golders Green crem, or his ashes were. 'It's bisexual history,' you told them, and they rolled their eyes but got their umbrella (BBC-branded, always so loyal). You knew their grandmother was there, too. 'And Bram Stoker,' you added, 'although he's more associated with Highgate Cemetery because of—' 'The Highgate Vampire, yes, I know,' and you see how your obsessions are centripetal rather than eccentric, always curling in upon, and around, themselves like the intercurved membraneous and bony labyrinths of the inner ear. They're holding the door with their virtual ID, calling back, come on, we can take the 13 from Portman Square. It took nearly an hour, and the crem was closed when you got there, stranding you in suburbia. You wondered what it was like when the smoke was rising.

And now you live near a decommissioned nuclear power station. Smoke rises everywhere. There was a story going around, before you lost network altogether, that the isles were ringed with smoke from the return to coal-fired power stations after Brexit and the permanent loss of Russian gas, a thick fog that cuts them – you, you suppose – off from the rest of the world. On a clear day here you can see forever, and you can see nothing like that, but you know there are no birds, so maybe it's true. There to here. You remember the arguments, coal versus nuclear. Pits grassed over and reopened by autonomous robots. Although the government claimed it would create jobs, they then said it was too dangerous for humans, then closed off entire communities, fenced them out because the robots, too, were dangerous. There were protests everywhere, against everything. Golders Greenham Common, you joked to your then-lover, as you passed the signs tied by faded ribbons outside the tube station.

They laughed and said, 'You know it's a bird habitat now, Greenham, one of the last sites for ground-nesting birds like linnets and nightjars.' You liked the word nightjar, had always liked the sound of Greenham Common, felt it resonate with you. As you fetch tins for the next week and secure the cache with both a digital keypad and an old bike chain, oiling it against the persistent sea-rust, you have this fragile, tensile feeling like a banner, wonder what it would have been like to be there. You were barely a child when the protestors embraced the base, tens of thousands of feminists laughing and climbing over barbed wire fences dressed as teddy bears, facing down soldiers and policemen with rifles.

Women who could set up benders in high winds, write songs, go to prison cheering: that's who you wanted to be. Who you are. When you first came here, the lighthouse was in such disrepair that you lived in a tent on the shingle for a few late summer weeks, your electric van parked up on the road and too full of boxes to be a decent kip. You'd pack it up every morning in case anyone caught you, but the tritium had sent everyone packing, and the razor wire prevented most other people. You hadn't been dressed as a teddy bear as you clambered over it, then dug under it, but you should have been. Once the boxes were through, your having found an old fisherman's barrow to drag them down the shingle, you covered the wire back up and told the car-sharing company to come and collect the van, which you'd driven to Lydd, a few miles away.

Digitise, boil, glue gun: vinyl sidings to line the worn-down planks in the winter. You feel criminal, doing this to the discs that gave you life, some given you by your grandparents, scratchy but still playable. Needs must. There are no building materials bar driftwood, and that is in short supply here. Something about longshore drift. You walk the endless, edgeless smooth of Camber Sands, finding little. Around the lighthouse you find sea kale, some sea buckthorn you pluck with care, evening primrose to press for tiny, hopeless drops of oil, wild parsnip and water mint. Not anymore. No birds, few bees. Nothing pollinated.

SO MAYER

You dream of them, the birds, the flowers. Wake in the cloudy moonlight and wonder whether others do too, whether there is a way to bring them from dreams back into reality. Like radio waves. Do the birds hear what you play? As if the podcast had uploaded to the clouds, you think you can hear it outside the window, 'I Never Stopped Loving You' by Anohni and OPN condensing like the rain that almost never falls here, which surely now qualifies as a desert and maybe not the only one of these isles. What had you emailed to Anohni to receive the track, what exchange did you make, words for words, sounds for sounds. You like to think of the messages still floating out there somewhere, floating being the operative word given the server farms' water usage.

Waves of sleep crash over you, and you dream or you wake and it's dawn, and you step out onto the beach, the shingle still wet from high tide, the moon and its gravity still extant, although you remember rumours that it was shifting. You hear a humming, the comforting sound of the desalinator you built in the perfect old bowl of the tanning copper. And above that, or curled within it, pitch-shifting within the drone, something, coming closer. At first you think the figures are birds, but then you realise they are far away, not small, and moving. The music you heard in the moonlight is getting louder, filling the air in a dispersed way, a kind of sound-pollen, swooping. There is a tinniness to it, an echo you can't quite place. You pull your patchwork dressing gown around you, your margravine garb, and press your feet in their vegan Docs into the stones. People.

TRUTH & DARE

There are people. They are. Dozens of them, hands extended. You recognise the echo now, the metallic sound of old mobile-phone speakers, all cued to play your podcast like a choir. They come in bright colours and dark, dressed as creatures and as themselves, a little ragged from the razor wire, carrying picnics and bottles and each other, the shingle having no route for a wheelchair. They are laughing, but you know it is not at you. You sit in your wooden chair, nailed together from the best pieces of driftwood and slung with a vinyl seat, slightly wavy but serviceable, and they circle around you, break over you like waves, calling your name.

You are not naïve, even in the dream, if this is a dream. You have seen the photographs of the queer filmmaker who lived here, what was his name, Jargon? Gorgon? You once knew it, knew people who knew him. Remember his videos for the Pet Shop Boys and This Mortal Coil, the – childhood feverdream – astounding moment that Elisabeth Welch appears in his *Tempest*, singing 'Stormy Weather' to an honour guard of hornpiping sailors. He made this place famous for a while, beloved of queers who left with sand in their pockets, under their packers, in their armpits, warm pits. Until the art–industrial complex took over his house and made it a private retreat, put up electrified fences that even you haven't been able to breach. But once he too sat on the shingle and was encircled, his face turned up to the sky as you are turning yours, listening.

But the voices pass you by and sweep down to the sea. They were not come to canonise you, they are calling you to join them. With the slowness of dream or early morning or age, you walk down to the shoreline where green sandpipers once hopped and you could watch Manx shearwaters, fearless, dive. They are not waiting for you, the people, with their piercings and shaved heads and weaves and undercuts and fringes and fauxhawks and beaded braids and top knots and wedges and blow-outs and rattails, many of which you have sported too at different points, before this long grey plait that whips against your back in the wind. Their hair greets you, their radiant faces turned to the sea as each of them reaches into a pocket or a bag or a bra cup or a boot-top.

Stones. Stones that were found, you understand, as they tell you with dream clarity, in charity shops and exhibitions, in mailboxes and moving boxes, then given to them by lovers and elders. Stones that once were here, were taken from here and passed on as mementoes, their atoms connected to the stones that remain. You realise, or are told, that you weren't hearing old phone speakers. That the stones, bodywarm, were resonating your broadcast. Are, the last notes of 'Ovid's Metamorphoses' receding towards the marsh on the sea-wind. You are holding such a stone in your hands too, a stone that you had picked up many years before, with another lover who had been passionate about gardens, the person who taught you how to make sea buckthorn jam without ripping your hands to pieces, who could grow anything, forage anything. Who gave you all the kisses, and died, and left you without mercy. Of course you are crying, holding this stone, her stone. The stone that brought you back here, fragment of memory, homing beacon, like the magnetite in birds' brains that directs their migrations. Not only you, no longer alone. Never alone.

Oh. Let it go. There is a not-quite-silence like the flutter of wings, like the whisper-song of the blue jay. We lift stones up on our palms, in our mouths, and – with a shiver and a stutter like variable-speed film, like that old nature documentary come to life, strange hybrid beasts, heartbeats stuttering in your hands – they shake out their various wings, open their beloved throats, and fly.

ACKNOWLEDGEMENTS

Thank you to Tobias Wray, Peter Scalpello, and Sarah Crewe for permission to include quotations from their gorgeous poems as epigraphs to, respectively, 'Silicon', 'diable', and 'goes to see'. Many of these stories were written, revised or developed at Arteles Creative Center in Finland, on a month-long writing residency. Huge thank yous to Teemu and Essi for the programme and the extraordinary privilege of your hospitality, and to my incredibly generous and brilliant fellow Artelesians: Allison, Audrey, Faiza, Iman, Lily, Masha (and Eulia Bea), Nesto, Sharone, Toby, and Tomás. You are all kneaded into these stories, especially 'House of Change'.

Residencies are incredible, and also most of the work was done while working: thank you to all the readers, writers, publishers and doggoes who visit Burley Fisher Books for their constant celebration of books and stories, and especially to my champion bookselling comrades Ant, Cat, Dan, Emma, Enya, Jason, Oisín, Pema, and Sam: legends only. Hey guys, 'corpus' is for you.

Over the seven years of its compilation, this book has been kept company by many others, and many films, songs, exhibitions, and thinking of all kinds. I cite many of these sources within the stories themselves, but 'to the light' is

ACKNOWLEDGEMENTS

particularly dependent on some crucial uncited sources, including many conversations with Adam Zmith for *The Film We Can't See*, with my Club Des Femmes co-conspirators Jenny Clarke, Ania Ostrowska and Selina Robertson, and with Georgeous Michael for his *Mädchen* drag performance. Thank you also to Aaron Lecklider for quoting Valentine Ackland's poem 'Teaching to Shoot (England, July, 1942)' in *Love's Next Meeting: The Forgotten History of Homosexuality and the Left in American Culture*; thank you to B. Ruby Rich, Richard Dyer, Jenni Olson and Chris Straayer for writing so passionately about *Mädchen in Uniform* and its baby butches; and thank you to Duncan Carson for the trove of poster art.

'green children' has its roots in a piece about libraries written for Charlotte Richardson Andrews' *Working Class Queers* zine. 'Lyonesses' appeared in the BSFA anthology *Fission* 1, with thanks to Allen Stroud, and to Cristina Jurado, who translated it into Spanish, asking amazing questions, for Celsius and *Windumanoth*. 'Pornographene' appeared in *Extra Teeth* 4, with thanks to Heather Parry who was, and is, absolutely right about the first line, among other incisive edits. 'ghost' includes some material previously published as 'Who You Gonna Call?' by Penned in the Margins' project *Electronic Voice Phenomena*. 'curse' appeared as 'what you do with a curse', a text and audiostory commissioned by Peter Aers for *a curse poem*, an online and stage collaboration at Vooruit, Ghent. 'Hot Mess Observation' develops some of the ideas from 'Listen to the State of Us', commissioned by Eoin Dara for *Ghost Calls* (Dundee Contemporary Art, 2021). 'zeus' appeared as a text

ACKNOWLEDGEMENTS

and audiostory as part of Something Other's tenth chapter, 'On Visions', with thanks to Mary Paterson, Maddy Costa, and Diana Damian Martin, and to Ignota for hosting the audio. 'Dune Elegies' was shortlisted for the 2023 Dinesh Allirajah Prize for short fiction, organised by Comma Press and the University of Central Lancashire; thank you to Jenny Chamarette for a first reading of that story.

First readers and their notes are the best. Adam Zmith for 'Pornographene', Tobias Wray for 'Silicon', SF Said for 'to the light' (and for the pun 'Foccaccia in the Rye' in 'corpus'), Sam Fisher for 'curse', and Faiza Hasan for 'Hot Mess Observation': you all had brilliant insights and generously allowed me to develop them as mine. Jemma Desai read an early version of 'vampire' and intuited that it wasn't ready, and why. Versions of 'zeus', 'ghost' and 'oestro junkie' (and a very different version of 'diable', which hybridises aspects of 'index' and 'out') first appeared on my tinyletter *Disturbing Words*. Thank you to all the online readers who read and sent thoughts, especially the person who wrote back to 'ghost', asking what it was I wasn't saying. Tom de Ville and Clem walked us up Mount Caburn and, alongside the amazing Queer Folk project, helped turn 'Listen to the State of Us' into 'Hot Mess Observation': here's to our Caburn crossover episode.

A million thanks and all the emoji to my pen-pals for their timely and timeless generosity and wisdom: Grace Barber-Plentie, Jason Barker, Sophie Brown, Maria Cabrera, Emily Carlton, Helen Charman, Theo Chiotis, Hyun Jin Cho, Anna Coatman, Sidney Coles, Corinn Columpar, Alison Croggon,

ACKNOWLEDGEMENTS

Will Forrester, Kate Hardie, Kat Hobbs, Daniel Heath Justice, Freddie and Issy Levy, Yen Ooi, Vanessa Peterson, Rebekah Polding, Nisha Ramayya, Rajni Shah, Elhum Shakerifar, Sarah Shin, Preti Taneja, Campbell X, and all those already named.

Cipher Press are a phenomenon, and make every aspect of the publishing process a punk pleasure. Massive thanks to Wolf for the absolutely perfect dream cover (and to Davina Silver and Leena Desai for encouraging me to go with the pink), and to Odhran O'Donoghue for an exquisite Post-it proof*read*. All remaining factual errors are either mine, or evidence we're in the wrong timeline.

To Jack and Ellis (and Sid): you make everything possible, and possible, everything.